How to Successfully kidnap Strangers

Max Booth III

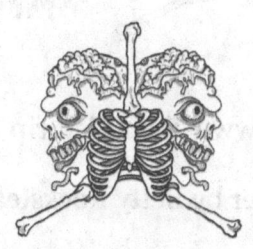

Ghoulish Books
San Antonio, Texas

How to Successfully Kidnap Strangers
Copyright © 2024 Max Booth III
First Edition 2015

Second Edition

All Rights Reserved

ISBN: 978-1-943720-97-2

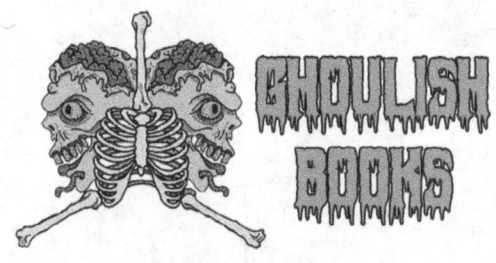

www.Ghoulish.rip

Cover by Betty Rocksteady

Also by Max Booth III

For Lori

1.
Phlegm for the Soul

ALL HARLAN ANDERSON wanted was a doughnut. A simple breakfast treat for a simple man who just wanted to relax all day and read shitty, pirated books on his eReader. Doughnuts and books were the essential elements of any paradise.

He'd gotten the eReader two years ago at a Christmas work party. A coworker had won it during the white elephant drawing and tossed it in the trash after the night was over, declaring "reading was for pussies". Harlan had waited until everybody else went home before he dug through the wastebasket and collected it. He found it underneath a barely touched slice of chocolate cake, which he also took home.

Reading was all Harlan had in life. His friends were nonexistent and the majority of his family was either dead, in jail, or simply uninterested. Books were his only real companions. Bad books, mostly. The kind of books that he didn't even like to read but he read anyway just so he could have a reason to bitch on Facebook. Books like Sergio Placid's *Eight Equals Zero,* or Nick Twig's *The Trampoline Incident.* So, any BILF Publishing book, really. Books I'd Like to Fuck Publishing. Jesus Christ. What a dumb company name. No wonder their books were trash.

Harlan walked into the coffee shop at eight in the morning, licking his lips at the pastry images on the menu above the barista. For a man who didn't socialize with people and spent the majority of his time at home, alone, the coffee shop was like a trip to Disneyland. He got to sit around with people who weren't being forced to be near him due to work-related activities and eat fatty snack foods while drinking overpriced coffee. Reading at home certainly had its benefits, such as the freedom to lay around in the nude, but he often preferred to do his reading in public. Sometimes, if he was sitting next to someone who was also alone, he'd attempt to engage the person in a conversation about how much he hated whatever it was he was currently reading. Sometimes strangers would actually respond and continue the discussion. Most of the time they'd stand up and walk away.

Today the coffee shop was playing the same Mumford & Sons song that was always on whenever he walked in the building. Sometimes the lyrics varied, but that didn't make the song any different. The walls were littered with inspiration quotes inaccurately credited to Hendrix and Einstein. There was only one person ahead of him in line, and he was taking his sweet time to order. The guy looked like he was on meth or some shit. His eyes were all black and crazed looking. The paranoid look of someone who hadn't slept in a decade. Words shot from his mouth like diarrhea from a flustered asshole, but not much of it was making any sense. Every few syllables, he would turn around and glare at Harlan, then turn back to the barista and attempt to finish his order. Eventually, the tweaker settled for a slice of lemon cake and fled the coffee shop.

"This city is full of degenerates," Harlan said to the barista as he approached the counter.

"What do you want?" She stared at him, showing no hint of amusement. She could have easily said 'What the *fuck* do you want?' and it would have better matched her tone.

"Hello?" The barista rolled her eyes. "Do you, like, uh, want anything or not?"

"Uh, a jelly doughnut, please. And a medium coffee, if that's okay."

She raised her pierced eyebrow at him, probably wondering why anyone would ask if it was okay to order a coffee inside a coffee shop. He paid and took his drink and doughnut to the lounge area, planning on sitting in one of the shop's recliner chairs and busting out his eReader. He'd illegally downloaded Sergio Placid's *The Cumming of Christ,* and he was looking forward to learning why an English teacher would ever be stupid enough to assign the book to his students as required reading, as was the case of the teacher up in Portland—who, understandably, was no longer employed.

Except he couldn't sit down, because all the tables in the coffee shop were currently occupied. He couldn't believe it. Tables were filled by dickheads in tie-dye beanies and teenaged girls finding their cell phones' G-spots. One table, a dirty, rancid old lady was just sitting there, eating her hair. Harlan stood next to her for a moment, hoping his presence would convince her to leave, but even when he cleared his throat she didn't seem to take the hint.

"Excuse me," he finally said, and tapped her shoulder. "*Excuse me.*"

The lady slowly lifted her head and smiled a toothless smile, then spit a glob of green phlegm in his face. Harlan screamed and fled the coffee shop, wiping his face off with the collar of his *Big Bang Theory* T-shirt. Gagging, he realized he'd dropped both his coffee and his doughnut inside the shop. Most of the coffee was on his shoes, burning his feet. He screamed a number of obscenities into the sky and flipped off God with his middle finger.

God responded with laughter.

No, not God. Just some guy standing behind him.

Harlan turned around. It was the tweaker who'd ordered the lemon pound cake. He pointed at Harlan. "Yo, didn't nobody ever tell you not to mess around with Crazy Rita? She's crazy, you know."

"No." He gagged again. "Nobody's ever told me."

The tweaker nodded furiously, still laughing. He reminded Harlan of the lunatic hitchhiker from *The Texas Chain Saw Massacre*. "Yeah, dude, lady owns this city. The mayor gave her a key. You know, one of them huge keys they give heroes and shit? Yeah. One of those. So she's allowed to go wherever she wants, eating hair and spitting in faces. It's like, her right as an American, you know?"

Harlan rubbed his shoe against the curb, cleaning some of the coffee off him. "I have to go home."

He tried walking away, but the tweaker jumped in front of him and held out his hands. "Wait, wait, wait. I just . . . I just got one question to ask you, real fast. Cool?"

Harlan shrugged, irritated. "What?"

"Is your name . . . Harlan?" The tweaker leaned forward, conspiratorial. "Is your name . . . Harlan Anderson?"

"Uh." Harlan stepped back, balancing on the edge of the curb. "Do I know you?"

The tweaker gave Harlan an apologetic look. "Yeah, dude, I think you do."

Then he tackled Harlan into the street.

His eReader flew out of his hands and soared through the sky. *The Cumming of Christ* would have to wait for another day.

2.

The Surreality of Reality

AT ONE POINT, Nick was positive the vomit on his face had been wet. Now, though, upon waking in the middle of who-fuckin'-knew-o'clock, the vomit was dry and pasted to his skin. But at least the odor had remained. And it provoked him to rush to the toilet and puke all over again. Afterward, he wetted a washcloth and cleaned his face off a little, then swished some mouthwash around his gums, savoring the burning sensation.

Maybe his brain had been replaced with one of those little cymbal monkeys and the little bastard was going nuts. Any other explanation for the current throbbing in his skull would be an understatement. He had no idea how much he drank last night, but clearly he had reached some sort of personal achievement.

Nick glanced down in the toilet and grimaced. Only about one third of the vomit had made it inside the bowl, and that was being generous. This was his apartment. He didn't have to clean up his own sick. That's why others stayed the night, so he could blame the mess on someone else and make them wipe it up. He whipped out his dick and pissed in the sink, watching his reflection in the mirror. His face could have been the toilet's ugly cousin.

There was a shit-ton of work he had intended on

getting accomplished today, but he knew, going by the way he was currently feeling, he wouldn't do a thing all day. Maybe he'd just hang out and play some X-Box. Fuck it.

Sometimes he pretended like he was going to slack off all day and not get anything done. But he never did. He'd joke around on Facebook about being a bum who spent his time jacking-off and watching reruns of *Veronica Mars,* but that was only because nobody wanted to hear about you spending ten straight hours staring at a Microsoft Word document. People could relate to laziness. You start talking about business, and napping sounds a little too appetizing.

Instead of playing X-Box, he'd take care of a few errands, come home, and immediately get to work. There was editing to finish. There was writing to start. Books didn't finish themselves. Every second he didn't spend progressing his publishing company and his own writing career was a second he might as well had spent in the grave.

There came a point when you were drowning in so many different projects with their own specific deadlines that reality as you understood it faded away. The projects piled up one after another, kind of like dishes gathering in a sink, a few at a time so you didn't really notice, but suddenly you were being swallowed by that great avalanche known as the Eternal Hustle.

The background of your workplace area chipped away like flecks of old paint. Nothing mattered besides the work. Food was forgotten, sometimes purposely due to lack of funds. Conversations were abandoned midsentence. Sleep was cashed in for extra hours on the clock. The world around you became insane. People started arguing about *True Detective* plagiarizing Ligotti when it was obviously just a case of influence and homage, but every time you considered weighing in your own opinion, you forgot what everybody was arguing about and you found yourself back in front of another goddamn project, because you just finished one workload and now another was nagging for attention.

Feed me, Seymore . . .

So you worked on the new project and your eyeballs dried out because you forgot to blink and your stomach committed suicide because you hadn't eaten in two days and none of it was important, none of it at all. The only thing that mattered was the next word you wrote, the next character you gave the gift of life.

You fled to your own private catacombs and locked the door behind you. Reality disintegrated and in its place stood a dream. A dream you experienced while awake, only you weren't really sure you were awake. You weren't really sure of anything anymore. You just hoped that once you finally did wake up—years from now, on your deathbed— the work you'd done wasn't complete and total shit.

But until then, there was more work to be done, and there was never not going to be work to be done while his heart continued to function, and the great wonderful truth was he wouldn't trade any of this for the world.

And even if his alcoholic agent wasn't able to sell his new novel, *The Owls in the City,* to one of the Big Five, or the Big Six, or the Big Dick, then Nick would continue self-publishing his books through his own small press, because in the end, it didn't really matter. The readers didn't care who published what. They just wanted something to help pass the time between life and death.

Nick returned to the living room. Louise was passed out on the floor, naked. He vaguely remembered her and Stephen fucking sometime last night, but Nick had fallen asleep before either of them finished. He scratched the lice in his scalp as he stared at her, then realized how creepy he would look if she suddenly woke up, and ran off into the kitchen to see if there was any food. There wasn't.

He was the founder of his own publishing company and he couldn't even afford a fucking Pop Tart.

He reached in his pocket for his cell phone, planning

on calling up Eliza and seeing if she wanted to buy him some burgers—Eliza never turned down a burger, and since she freelanced for multiple small presses, she actually could afford food once in a while—when he realized his phone was missing. He checked his bed. It wasn't there.

It took him a few minutes to remember he'd thrown it at the bartender last night at Nightscapes. The guy had been an ultra-Christian dickhead and kept loudly disapproving of Nick and his authors' behavior, so he'd chucked his phone at him. In retrospect, there were probably better objects to whirl at a bartender. Objects that Nick didn't own and depend on daily. Like an astray, or the tray of peanuts on the bar that had begun to spout some kind of parasite. Now Nick would have to go back down there and see if they had saved the phone or thrown it away. Even if they did somehow have his phone, it was probably shattered or, at the very least, sticky and gross.

"Shit."

Nick dry swallowed some aspirin, got dressed, and drove toward Nightscapes, hoping he hadn't been banned for life—although if he had, he'd understand. You didn't toss dildo crucifixes at a crowd of strangers and not face any consequences.

Indent Your Face

NOBODY KNEW HOW to indent a paragraph. Writers stared at their screens with an assortment of indentation choices, all of them wrong except for one. The answer was available online—all they had to do was Google the question. It wasn't like they weren't checking Facebook and YouPorn every other ten minutes, anyway.

But no, looking up common manuscript formatting guidelines was apparently too much to ask from a profession as embarrassing as "writer". So they did what they always did and clicked the goddamn TAB key. Eliza couldn't conceive of a more selfish action, besides the rare fuckheads who actually used the *space* key three or four times to indicate an indentation. She firmly believed that it should be legal to scalp such a dubious thick-skinned motherfucker.

Sometimes she was afraid of meeting a "space-indent" author in person, because she really didn't know what she'd do. She suspected she'd go into some sort of blind rage, like how Vietnam vets go all batshit whenever a balloon pops and they start shooting fools with antique rifles and gutting them with bayonets, or whatever they used in Vietnam. Like Eliza ever paid attention to that shit.

Like there weren't more important things to be doing in high school than paying attention to some bored middle-aged man talk about wars that had ended before she was even alive.

If it was up to Eliza, BILF Publishing would automatically reject any author who submitted to them without using the proper indentation formatting on their manuscript. If these people didn't care enough to make their work presentable, then why should she care enough to edit it?

To her, it spoke plenty about the type of author the person would be. If the author couldn't pay attention to a few simple guidelines, then how could anyone honestly expect the author to take his or her work seriously? The type of assholes who didn't care about indentation etiquette were the same type of assholes who did zero self-promotion besides once in a while posting links on their Facebook pages with the "pls buy my book lol" captions. Shit, they were the same type of assholes who posted about every new five-star review they received from their parents. This business was stressful enough without them involved in it—adding them into the equation was like a hammer bashed into an already livid migraine.

If it was up to Eliza, they would all be executed. Literally executed. Brains blown out all over their impotent keyboards.

What she needed right now was a break. She'd been formatting this book for the last four hours and if she messed with it any longer without getting a burger in her system, she'd drive her tiny fist through her stupid laptop. The final proof for Tommy Yorke's *Cock Mutants* wasn't due for another two weeks, anyway. She just liked to get a head-start whenever possible. In the past, her typical work schedule had involved digesting as many drugs as her friends could afford to offer for free and waiting until the day before a deadline to even start a project. But she'd stopped partying so hard once her parents kicked her out and she had to actually start coming up with rent money once a month. That wasn't to say she was a total spaz or anything. She still enjoyed the occasional acid trip and casual orgy.

Eliza didn't have a car, and she had too much shit to do to just start walking around town, so she pulled out her cell phone—more like lifted it from her desk because who doesn't always have their cell phones out, in reach, just in case someone wants to contact you or you witness something extraordinary that you just *have* to record on video?—and called her brother.

He answered on the eighth ring.

"Who is this?"

"Your cell has caller ID, Billy. You know who this is."

"My screen's dirty. Can't see shit."

"Have you thought about cleaning it?"

"I tried that once. The phone was destroyed."

"That's because you tried washing it in the sink."

"How the fuck was I supposed to know?"

Eliza groaned. She rubbed her stomach. "Look, I'm hungry as balls over here. Come pick me up and I'll treat you to a burger."

"Uh."

"Billy?"

"Now's not really a good time."

"Oh, shut up. You're never doing anything. Come get me."

"No, really, sis, now's not a good time. I have some . . . shit going on."

"I'll even buy you a milkshake."

"Uh."

"Billy . . . ?"

"I don't know, sis."

"Dude, get your ass over here."

"Fuck. All right. Give me a few minutes."

Eliza placed the phone back on her desk and stared at the opened InDesign file on her laptop. She couldn't have forced herself to continue working right now if her life was on the line. Screw it. She minimized InDesign and brought up her browser, which directed her straight to Facebook. Three private messages were waiting in her inbox. The first one was from some author she'd never heard of asking if she was interested in reading and reviewing his book in exchange for a free PDF copy. She blocked the person without responding. The second private message was sent from a barely dressed teenager asking Eliza if she liked girls who squirted. The last private message was from Tommy Yorke:

"hey grrrll i decided to go thru and change my POV to first person present tense after all, so i guess u need this version now? thnx!"

He'd included a Word attachment of *Cock Mutants Final FINAL Draft*.

Eliza closed her laptop and screamed.

4.
Officer Doughnut

OFFICER JOSEPH NOUS was fully aware he was supporting a stereotype by accepting a free doughnut from the coffee shop, but honestly, he didn't give a shit. Doughnuts were delicious no matter who you were or what your job was. If bystanders shouted any smartass remarks, he'd just douse the fuckers with pepper spray and claim they were reaching for his gun.

Joseph nodded at the doughnut and smiled at the girl behind the counter, told her thanks and mentioned what a big help she was being. She smiled back and winked. Her flirting was obvious. Especially since she kept trying to give him her phone number in case he had any further questions, despite him not even being finished with his initial set of questions.

He swallowed a chunk of his doughnut and continued. "As you were saying, Ms. Matthews?"

The girl shrugged. "Like I said, that crazy bitch spat in the dude's eye, he freaked out and ran outside, and that was all I really noticed. I was kinda busy making coffee, which is, ya know, like my job? But yeah. Like. Okay. Get this. When the man was in line, like, waiting? There was this other dude ahead of him, and he was acting all buggy, like he was tripping? Kept looking back at the other man like he knew him or something. So I guess I wouldn't be surprised if he was the one who was fighting him outside. I mean, like, who else could it have been?"

"Uh huh."

Joseph had his notebook open, but he wasn't writing any of this down. He'd already gotten the gist of the story from the bystanders outside. One man randomly approached another man, had a brief exchange of words, then they attacked each other. They fought in the middle of the street, bashing their fists into each other's faces, until a car came along and blasted on the horn. Then one man, the crazy one who'd initiated the assault, dragged the driver out of the car and started beating on him, too. When the original victim began crawling away, the crazy man ran back over to him, grabbed him by his hair, and dragged him to the car. The psycho then popped open the driver's trunk, tossed his first victim and the driver inside, closed it, got behind the wheel, and drove away.

All this time, a crowd of pedestrians stood and recorded the brawl on their cell phones. The video was currently on YouTube with over thirty thousand views already. Everything was a TV show now. Something unusual happened and instead of helping, people would just insert a screen between them and the bizarre. Cell phones became coping mechanisms. They made the horror of reality less real. Less tangible. As long as they stayed far enough to capture everything on video, then danger remained a fairy tale. The world was insane and surreal. Of course, that wasn't entirely true, because someone *did* attempt to help the man being assaulted, and look what happened to him. Not only was he also beaten, but then he was kidnapped to top it all off. Nobody was truly safe. Maybe the people with their cell phones had the right idea. Stay back, film the action, then upload it on the Internet for the whole world to drool over. This was the way of life now. This was the law of disorder.

But goddamn, this was one fine doughnut.

HOW TO SUCCESSFULLY KIDNAP STRANGERS

When he left the coffee shop, Joseph made sure he had saved the barista's phone number. Maybe there would be more free pastries in the near future. Or maybe she wasn't interested in him at all. He'd been delusional before, with other girls. Sometimes women were nice to him just because they were paranoid he'd discover drugs in their purses. It was difficult to determine who was kissing his ass and who was genuinely attracted to him. His last relationship hadn't made it two months. She told him she was a stripper and nothing more, which turned out to be bullshit when Joseph busted her for hooking behind her place of employment. And the girlfriend before the stripper had only started having sex with him because she thought she'd be able to talk him into stealing drugs from the evidence room. Once she realized he wasn't going to budge on that issue, she gave another officer on his precinct a blowjob and convinced him to do what Joseph refused.

He drove away from the coffee shop wondering if he was destined to live life alone. Well, not completely alone. His precious dachshund, Lucy, was waiting for him at home. As long as he continued to feed and pet her, she would always love him. And maybe that was enough.

5.
Burgers & Milkshakes

BILLY WAS HIGH as fuck. It was obvious as soon as Eliza got in the passenger seat. Dude was shaking and twitching and acting like the sky was raining black helicopters. His eyes were dark and his skin was bloodied from persistent scratching.

Plus, he wasn't driving his own car.

"Whose car is this?"

"This is the car of Jesus Christ, our Lord and Savior."

"And he just let you borrow it, huh?"

Billy nodded. "Jesus and me are tight, yo."

"You look fucked-up, man," she said, feeling a mixture of amusement and worry. "What have you taken?"

Billy kept scratching his face and wincing like it burned. "Last night, or last year, after the bar, I left everybody and was hanging out with some preacher, I don't know. He had some good shit, sis. Not even playin'. Like Walter White shit, yo. Like the kinda shit the Burger King Queen has, but this was actually decent. Haven't been to sleep in days, in centuries. I've been awake since the Big Bang, sis. Maybe I am the cause of all life on Earth—shit, who knows, right?"

"Crank?" Eliza dug her nails into her palms. "C'mon, Billy, not that hardcore shit again. We talked about this."

HOW TO SUCCESSFULLY KIDNAP STRANGERS

"Well, I'm a hardcore motherfucker, yo."

"Mom didn't stop helping you take a bath until you were thirteen."

"I was afraid of getting shampoo in my eyes. Jesus. You know that."

"How long have you been awake?"

"I have no concept of time right now."

His hands were shaking on the steering wheel. Eliza gulped. "Maybe I should drive."

Billy laughed. "You're not insured for this car."

"And you are?"

"I told you. Me and Jesus are tight."

"Whatever, man. Let's just go to Sonic already. I need some meat inside me."

Billy opened his mouth, but Eliza smacked his chest before he had a chance to say anything.

"Don't you fucking dare."

Billy grumbled something unintelligible and started the car. As they drove toward Sonic, Eliza heard something loud and heavy thumping from the trunk. The sound was drowned out by Billy raising the volume on the car radio. One of the only five good Metallica songs was playing.

They pulled up to Sonic and Billy ordered their food. He held out his hand for Eliza to give him the money, but she just smiled and shook her head. Like she'd trust him to handle her cash. She'd fallen for that kind of shit before, but not anymore. He was too out of his mind to show any disappointment in her distrust for her own sibling. When the Sonic girl came rolling out on her skates, Eliza motioned for her to come around to the passenger side, and she paid her directly.

Eliza loved her brother and all, but he was just one of those people you couldn't trust. And it wasn't even the drugs that made him that way. Hell, Eliza did drugs and she managed to be responsible with money. She managed not to rob people. Of course, she didn't do the kind of drugs her brother favored. She stuck with weed, molly, mushrooms—mostly harmless shit. She didn't screw around with crank or heroin. She wasn't suicidal. She just liked to have fun. The crap Billy took, that wasn't fun. That was writing your own death sentence. But with that in mind, the drugs didn't cause his tendency to steal, despite what every politician and stuck-up asshole might have thought. Billy was just a thief by nature. Always had been. She remembered when they were kids and the little shit had broken her bedroom lock off while she was on a date. When she returned home, she discovered all of her books opened and her piggy bank shattered on the ground. No money in sight. And he was only like, what, nine when that happened? Dude had only gotten better at his craft. He was the kind of guy who wouldn't hesitate to swipe a waitress's tip off an uncleaned restaurant table. The kind of guy who'd reach into a panhandler's cup and take money out instead of drop any inside. She was not proud of his actions, but he was still her brother, and as much as she hated admitting it, she still cared about him. Their parents couldn't give two shits about them, so she was all he had—and, sadly, vice versa.

Now she sat there watching him inhale his burger, like he hadn't eaten in days, but instead of making her feel sad, like it probably should have, it just made her hungrier. She started opening the wrapping on her own burger when she heard the pounding from the trunk again. From the trunk of a car that she'd never seen Billy drive until today.

Shit.

"Billy, whose car did you say this was, again?"

Billy shrugged, smiling that smile he always did whenever he was guilty of something but didn't want to talk about it. Only this time, lettuce from his burger was sticking between his teeth, and mayonnaise was dripping down his chin, fusing with his trailer trash stubble and radioactive acne.

The pounding in the trunk grew louder and faster. Then the sound evolved from a muffled thud to a man screaming for help.

HOW TO SUCCESSFULLY KIDNAP STRANGERS

"Billy, whose fucking car is this?" she asked again, but Billy was forcing the last few bites of his burger down his throat and starting up the engine, backing up without looking behind him and burning rubber against cement as he shot out of the parking lot. The screaming grew louder.

"I may have screwed up," Billy finally said.

Eliza sat back in the passenger seat and closed her eyes, pretending she was back home in her comfy pajamas, behind her laptop, outlining various scalping strategies for those who didn't properly indent their manuscripts.

6.

Trunk Carcasses

"WHAT THE FUCK is going on?"

"I don't know."

"Who the fuck *was* that guy?"

"I don't know."

"What do you mean, *you don't know?*"

"I mean, I don't know."

"But you guys were fighting."

"Doesn't mean I know him, though, now does it?"

"So, what, you two just started fighting for no reason?"

"It seems that way."

"Well, what happened?"

"I don't know. He randomly attacked me on the street."

"That guy was small. How the hell do you reckon he fought both of us *and* lifted us into my trunk?"

"Drugs, probably. Who knows. Who cares?"

"I guess nobody. Where is he taking us?"

"How the hell should I know?"

"I thought you knew him."

"Christ, you're stupid."

"Hey, fuck you, buddy. Forgive me for being a little disoriented after being punched in the face and locked in my own goddamn trunk. I'm not even done finishing off the payments on this thing, and it's already been stolen twice now."

"How did it get stolen the first time?"

"I accidentally left the keys in the ignition when I stopped at a gas station. A nearby clown hopped in and took off."

"Get the fuck out of here. A clown?"

"Yeah. Head-to-toe, full clown get-up. I guess he'd just gotten off his shift at some carnival or something and was walking home when he noticed my ride. When they recovered it, every square inch of the interior was covered in confetti. I still haven't gotten all of it out."

"Jesus Christ."

"Yeah, man. Clowns are assholes."

"Why does it smell so badly in here? What do you keep in your trunk?"

"I . . . uh, I don't see how that's any of your business."

"What's in this bag?"

"You leave my bag alone. It's of no concern to you."

"You're pretty touchy."

"You're the one touching things."

"Calm down."

"That's kind of hard."

"Now, shut up, just listen. I'm thinking, despite me not knowing him, this guy *does* know me."

"How so?"

"He knew my name."

"But you don't know him?"

"Never seen him before in my life."

"What's your name, then?"

"I'm Harlan. You?"

"Lewis."

"Well, I'd say it was a pleasure to meet you, maybe under different circumstances . . . "

"Where do you think this guy's taking us?"

"I don't know. He doesn't seem to like me too much, though."

"I don't have time for this. I have places to be."

"And I don't?"

"Do you frequently piss off strangers?"

"Probably. This is the first time somebody's ever acted out on it, though."

"Do you think he's going to kill us?"

"Probably, yeah."

"Shit."

"I know."

"Man, you can't just tell somebody that."

"Didn't you see the crazy look in his eyes? He would have probably killed me on the street if you hadn't interrupted him. Now he'll kill you, too."

"Shit."

"Maybe we can pound on the roof some more, maybe scream a little louder."

"Do you think that'll help?"

"Probably not."

"Hmm. Let's do it, anyway."

7.
Beer Shits

"YOUR NIPPLES ARE HARD."

Louise woke up, mouth tasting like a mixture of hard liquor and male ejaculate, and she made a mental note to write a bizarro detective novel called *Rum & Cum*. It could be a sequel to her previous book, *Grits & Clits*.

Stephen sat on the couch, staring at her. He had a mostly empty bottle of beer in his lap, resting next to his crotch. She wondered if he had actually drunk the beer or if he'd dumped half into the sink to keep up the false persona of a hardcore alcoholic. Stephen didn't even like beer.

"I said your nipples are hard," he said.

"No shit. It's freezing in this apartment."

""Do you know where Billy went?"

"You just saw me wake up two seconds ago. Why would I know?"

"I just wondered."

"Did you actually drink that beer, or are you wasting them again?"

Stephen's cheeks turned red. "Don't you have a book deadline?"

"I'd prefer not to think about that."

"Yeah, until Nick's getting on your ass about it, asking why it isn't done yet."

"Would you be okay with that?"

"Okay with what?"

"With Nick on my ass."

"Oh fuck you."

"Maybe later." Louise yawned and scratched her crotch. "I have to take a dump first."

"You're one classy chick."

"That's why I make the big bucks."

Louise stood in the bathroom a moment, debating if she really wanted to clean up the vomit that had made itself present all over the toilet. Seriously, just everywhere. The bowl, the lid, the tank, even the wall behind the toilet. Just looking at it all almost induced her own offering of puke. She turned around and left the bathroom before she contributed to the mess.

"You didn't even flush," Stephen said as she passed. She responded with a middle finger.

Louise threw on some clothes, wincing at the cramp in her stomach. Fucking beer shits, they were the worst. They snuck up on you like a rattlesnake in the desert, slithering up to your boot and waiting to pounce upon your ankle. Maybe she shouldn't have drunk so much last night. Maybe she should have never stopped drinking. She could've forced herself to stay awake and drink until her death. Drink until she made her decomposed parents proud. Now her old man was a drunk worth aspiring to. He always said the best cure for a hangover was more alcohol. She'd tried that once and just started vomiting inside the beer bottle.

She would never have the liver of a dirty old man, and sometimes this was the most depressing realization in the world. Gone were Louise's dreams of being the new Bukowski. When she was younger, she'd lock herself in her room and reread Buk's entire bibliography. Ol' Hank was her first crush. She'd hide under blankets and masturbate to his nasty, ugly words. Ugly was the new pretty. She didn't want people to tell her she was beautiful. She wanted to be vile. She wasn't happy until onlookers were grimacing. Dirt was sexy. Bloody fingernails were hot as fuck. Heart-shaped candies and red roses were not.

"You wanna come with me to the gas station?" she asked, zipping her jeans.

"What for?"

"I'm not using the bathroom here. It's too disturbing. Plus, we can get some cappuccinos."

"What happened in the bathroom?" Stephen stood up and headed toward it, but Louise grabbed his shoulder and held him back.

"The Lord of Darkness wouldn't even step foot in that bathroom. Trust me, dude."

He rubbed his head. "Ugh. Last night was crazy. What I remember, at least."

"Not much to remember. We drank, we laughed, we threw dildos at strangers, then we came home and you fell asleep on top of me."

"Oh." He looked at his feet for support, but they didn't offer any. "Sorry about that."

"Whatever. That's why God gave me fingers, right?"

"I . . . I guess."

"So, gas station? Yes or no?"

"You paying?"

"Nobody's paying. That dude with the huge nose is the cashier in the mornings, the one who wants to bang me."

"Oh, okay, cool. Maybe we can score some muffins, too."

"Hell yeah, son."

8

Previously on How To Successfully Kidnap Strangers

BILLY SPED THROUGH town with no apparent destination in mind. Normally Eliza would lecture him on his driving, but she was too distracted with the whole "body in the trunk" dilemma. There were a few bites left of her burger, but she was no longer hungry. She dropped the remainder of her food in the Sonic bag and balled it up at her feet. Confetti littered the car floor. What the hell?

She groaned, wishing she'd never called her brother today. She should've just stayed home, kept formatting and boiled some Ramen.

"What do you mean, you 'kidnapped somebody'?" she asked, thinking maybe she was just hearing him wrong, thinking maybe she was asleep and this was all some stupid dream, thinking this couldn't possibly be happening.

"I feel that's pretty self-explanatory."

"Billy, seriously, who is in the trunk?"

Billy stayed quiet for a moment, like he was in deep concentration.

Eliza rolled her eyes. "Don't tell me you've forgotten."

"I just need to think for a moment."

"Where are we going?"

He shrugged. "I have no idea."

"Who is in the trunk?"

"Now, sis, you can't get mad . . ."

"Billy, who the fuck is in the fucking trunk?"

"Harlan Anderson."

Eliza laughed before she realized she was laughing. "No he fucking isn't."

Billy nodded.

She let his silence sink in and listened to the thumping from the trunk. Billy was serious.

"How did this even happen?" she asked.

Billy shrugged. "One thing after another, you know?"

"No, Billy, I don't fucking know, that's why I'm asking you."

"Okay, so, like I said, after last night at the bar, I left everybody and went off to this different party. We stayed up all night doing . . . you know, stuff. Then I left to get us all some coffee and cakes. And I'm standing in line, trying to decide what to get, and the motherfucker comes strolling in like he owns the joint."

"How did you even know it was him?"

"I just knew, okay? We've seen his stupid, smug-ass face on his blog before. Come on now. It's him."

"Then what happened?"

"Well, he's standing behind me in line, right? And he's just acting like a total asshole to everybody."

"How so?"

"Hmm. Okay, maybe he was just waiting patiently in line. Whatever. He's still an asshole. So, anyway, I got a lemon pound cake and left."

"How uneventful."

"No, dammit, listen. So, I'm waiting outside, eating my cake, watching the fucker through the window. And he's trying to find a place to sit down, right? And, okay, now get this, all right, so he's trying to sit down at this one table where Crazy Rita's at. You know Crazy Rita."

"Yeah." Bitch was crazy.

"Yeah, right, so he's talking to her, maybe he's asking her if he can sit down, maybe he's asking for a blowjob, who the fuck knows? Regardless, Crazy Rita takes one look at him and spits in his face."

Billy started laughing hysterically. Given different circumstances, Eliza might have joined him. But her stomach was knotted up with dread. She'd always been the more responsible one. Growing up, when they were getting high and leaping off sheds, she always aimed for trampolines or swimming pools. Billy would just fly for concrete. Cement in the ground and cement in the head.

"Billy? What happened then?"

"Right, okay. So Crazy Rita spits in his face and he starts freaking the fuck out, right? Drops his coffee and comes running out of the shop, just screaming and way overplaying the whole situation. Although, to be fair, I probably acted the same the first time Crazy Rita spit in my face."

Eliza nodded. "We all do."

"Yeah, right? It's like a rite of passage or something. Or a write. Like, you know, with a double you. Heh. Oh, speaking of, have you heard from Nick about royalties? I'm fucking broke as shit, spent the rest of my cash last night at that party. I'm pretty sure *Attack of the Chlamydia Kamikazes* has sold at least ten copies, easy. Well, at the very least, I know Mom bought a copy. She showed me the receipt."

"Billy, you're getting side-tracked. What happened next?"

Billy paused for a moment like he'd completely forgotten what they were talking about, then he smacked himself in the face. "Oh! Yeah. Right. Okay, so Harlan comes out screaming, and I'm standing there watching him, so I walk up to him and I'm like, 'Yo, are you Harlan

Anderson?' and he's like, 'What's it to you, cocksucker?' So I'm all like, 'Yo, how 'bout some fuckin' manners?' and he's all like, 'Suck my cock, you cocksucking cocksucker.' So, I'm all like, 'Prepare to die!' And then I started beating the shit out of him."

"Did anybody see you guys?"

"Well, yeah, there was a huge crowd. That's why I picked him up and got the hell out of there, before the police showed up."

"Why didn't you just leave him there?"

"I don't know, sis. It was all in the heat of the moment."

Eliza sighed. This was going to be a long fucking day. "So, is this his car, then?"

"Nah."

"Well. Whose car is it?"

"I have no idea."

"How can you not know?"

Billy shrugged. "I don't fucking know, okay? I mean, the driver's in the trunk and all, but I don't *know* him or anything."

"I thought you just said this wasn't Harlan's car."

"Right."

Eliza let that sit for a moment, pondering the situation. Then it clicked.

"Holy shit, Billy, how many fucking people are in the trunk right now?"

Blue Balls for Jesus

AFTER BRIEFING THE detectives with the information he'd collected, Officer Joseph Nous continued his patrol. He was looking forward to idling at a speed-trap and reading his copy of Sergio Placid's *The Cumming of Christ*.

The free doughnut the barista had given him was settling nicely in his stomach. He kept thinking that he didn't eat enough doughnuts, being a cop. He should have received free food every day, yet this was a first. Nobody ever treated him with respect. It was always "fuck the police" this and "kill all cops" that. Joseph had never done anything to anybody. Maybe that made him a bad cop. But then again, maybe that made him the best cop.

He arrived at his speed-trap, blasted the air conditioning, and opened up his wrinkled copy of *The Cumming of Christ*. The book was disgusting and obscene and he couldn't get enough of it. He'd never read anything so insane in his life. If he'd been introduced to these kinds of books when he was a kid, he would've definitely read more growing up. Maybe the same could be said for a lot of the kids of his generation. It wasn't a lack of interest in reading altogether, it was just a lack of interest in the same old vanilla school-friendly crap teachers forced onto their students. If someone had handed Joseph a copy of *The*

HOW TO SUCCESSFULLY KIDNAP STRANGERS

Cumming of Christ when he was ten, reading would have had a whole new meaning to him. Maybe he would have pursued education after high school. Maybe he wouldn't be some lame cop with nobody to love him but a wiener dog.

His speed-trap was between two abandoned fast-food restaurants. Before he began parking here, the spot was primarily inhabited by drug dealers and prostitutes. But thanks to his recent presence, they'd all scattered elsewhere to perform the inevitable. His squad car was like a mobile "no crime zone" flag. People avoided him more than they did the homeless psychos located on nearly every street corner of this city. Being a cop was the best occupation for anybody who just wanted to be left the hell alone. And Joseph did indeed want to be left the hell alone. He didn't enjoy having to confront people. How was he to know if somebody was packing a gun or a blade? Hell, even a needle would do the trick. Anybody could have a warrant out on their arrest. Nobody wanted to go to jail. Most people would do whatever it took to escape imprisonment, and that included shooting police officers in their faces.

The fast-food restaurants had been an Arby's and a McDonald's, and they'd closed down on the same day. A few years back, it was discovered that the employees at both establishments had been dealing various drugs through their drive-thrus by using elaborate code systems hidden in meal orders. Arby's grew increasingly frustrated with the low deals given by McDonald's, which stole most of their customers. One day, after the announcement of a $20 family pack meal of two quarter pounders, two fries, and twenty chicken nuggets, the fry cook of Arby's propped open the drive-thru window and opened fire at their competitor. McDonald's did not hesitate in returning the favor. It was a complete bloodbath and utter embarrassment to the fast-food industry. Both businesses shut down immediately and moved on to new locations. Nobody seemed to have the guts to rent out the buildings, so there they sat, infested with bullet holes and abandoned hamburger buns now a part of an undiscovered species of fungi. It was rumored the Burger King down the street had taken on the leftover drug clientele.

Someone knocked on the driver's window and Joseph nearly screamed. Heart beating fast, he turned to the side, expecting to find himself face-to-face with the muzzle of a pistol. Instead, he found a young girl standing outside his car, smiling. She was dressed in a yellow blouse and couldn't have been any older than fourteen or fifteen. He rolled down his window.

"Hi, there. Is everything okay?"

The girl laughed, blushing. She looked behind her, then turned back toward him. "I was just wondering if . . . uh . . . well, I was just wondering if you'd want to marry me."

"Excuse me?"

She continued giggling. Behind her, across the parking lot, someone else started laughing. The girl shook her head. "I'm sorry. My friend dared me to ask you that."

Joseph tried to laugh, but the realization that this little girl would probably be the only female to ever propose to him hit like a brick to the gut. "Very cute," he said. "I'd love to marry you."

The girl raised her fist to the air and shouted, "Yes!" Then she noticed the paperback in Joseph's hands and her eyes widened at the extremely graphic front cover. "Oh my God."

Joseph closed the book and threw it on the passenger seat. "No, it's not what you think."

The girl shook her head in disgust. "You sick fuck." She ran across the parking lot, giggling with her friend about the perverted cop reading porno books.

Joseph considered chasing after her and trying to explain himself, but decided it would only make matters worse. He picked up *The Cumming of Christ* and resumed reading. He made it two sentences in before his radio went

HOW TO SUCCESSFULLY KIDNAP STRANGERS

berserk. Apparently there was some type of brawl going on down at the Pic-n-Pac. And he was the closest officer to the gas station, so it was his lucky day.

He dropped the paperback on the passenger seat again and drove away, disappointed. He was really looking forward to reading about Jesus Christ's pornography career.

10.
There's No Such Thing
as a Free Cappuccino

AS IT TURNED OUT, the cashier with the huge nose who wanted to bang Louise no longer worked at the Pic-n-Pac. He'd been fired a few days ago after his assistant manager caught him violating a Hostess cupcake.

Louise hadn't noticed the huge-nosed cashier's absence until she attempted to walk out of the gas station with two cappuccinos and a shit-ton of muffins. A cashier, a woman with a perfectly normal-sized nose, shouted, "Hey! You haven't paid for that!"

Louise paused at the door, taking her time to turn around. Stephen was behind her, holding his own share of muffins, looking at her and mouthing, "Oh shit."

The cashier walked toward them, pointing and shouting. "Who do you think you are? You can't just walk in here, grab whatever you want, and leave without paying."

"Why not?" Louise asked, biting down on a muffin. She figured she was already busted, so fuck it, might as well have some fun.

The cashier seemed dumbstruck by her ignorance. "Because . . . it's against the law. You're stealing."

Louise shrugged. "Well, I never agreed to that law." She finished off her muffin and watched crumbs fall to the floor. Louise wondered if she should feel guilty, since somebody would have to eventually sweep that up, but decided that if this dumb bitch with the normal-sized nose hadn't interrupted her in the first place, then Louise would have waited to eat until she was outside the gas station.

"I'm calling the cops," the cashier said.

"Wait, wait, wait," Stephen said, trying to smile the same kind of sad puppy dog smile he used whenever he was trying to guilt Louise into anal. "This is all just a misunderstanding."

The cashier raised her eyebrow, ready to disbelieve any bullshit he was about to make up. "How so?"

"Uh, well, Louise here—"

"Don't use my real name, jackass."

Stephen gave her an ugly glare, then looked back at the cashier with his "can I puh-puh-puhleaze put it in your poop chute?" look. "I mean, uh, Betty, she thought I had already paid for the stuff, and I thought *she* had already paid for the stuff. It was a simple case of miscommunication, I can assure you. Of course we'll pay for all this. Right, Louise? I mean, Betty."

"Sure," Louise said. "If you have money."

Stephen broke his innocent persona. "I thought you had money."

"I never said that."

"Well, shit."

Stephen threw one of his muffins at the cashier. It missed her completely and smashed into a small child's face behind her. He fell down for the count, crying his stupid little head off. The boy's father, standing well over six feet tall and wearing motorcycle gang threads, turned around to face the cause of his son's unexpected muffin attack.

"Well, shit," Stephen said again.

The motorcycle guy stormed across the gas station,

pushed the normal-nosed cashier out of the way, and glared at them.

"Did you just throw a muffin at my son?"

Stephen stood there for a moment, holding in his breath and trying to avoid eye contact. Louise noticed the biker's hands balling into fists. She also noticed his brass knuckles.

"He sure did," Louise said. "And now I'm going to throw a hot cappuccino in his father's face."

He looked at Louise, confused. "What?"

Then he gasped as the hot liquid splashed into his eyes. He started screaming and backing up, then tripped over his own son. The boy let out of a wet, disgusting fart as his father squished his body with his weight.

"Holy shit," Stephen said. "That was hardcore."

"Fuck yeah it was," Louise said, feeling horny.

"I'm calling the police!" the cashier screamed, scrambling for the phone by the register.

"Uh, we should probably go," Stephen said.

"Fuck that," Louise said. "I'm not making this all be for nothing."

"What are you talking about?"

"I'm getting another cappuccino."

"Christ, you're crazy."

"Crazy in love!" she shouted, laughing and running to the cappuccino machine.

"Oh shit, Louise, the cops are here."

"Crap. Already?"

"I have some . . . stuff in my pocket, Louise. This isn't good."

"Relax, we're cool," she said, joining him with two more cappuccinos. "Let's get a-goin', honey badger."

"Please don't call me that."

"Whatever."

They walked outside the gas station just as the cop was getting out of his squad car. He was a huge son of a bitch, and when he was finally out of the vehicle, the car's suspensions lifted up and relieved themselves like a fat gut relaxing over a newly loosened belt buckle on Thanksgiving night. He rushed toward them and Louise pointed inside the store.

"Oh, Officer, you have to do something! There's a crazy biker in there attacking everybody! I think he has a gun!"

"Step aside, miss," the cop said. "I'll handle this."

Louise gave Stephen a look like she couldn't believe that had actually worked. Then she handed him one of the new cappuccinos and told him to get his ass in the car.

"I'm never going anywhere with you again," he said, once they were a safe distance from the gas station.

"Oh, come on," Louise said. "You know that was hella fun."

11.
God's Fluffer

NICK PULLED INTO the parking lot of Nightscapes and sat there for a moment, listening to the radio without actually paying any attention to it. He was thinking about last night and what happened at this same bar. It was bad enough to make him consider that maybe he should slow down on the drinking. At least for a while.

It had started out innocently enough. Him, Louise, Stephen, Billy, and Sergio all piled into his car around eight o'clock and drove down, making it with a good fifteen minutes to spare before Sergio's scheduled reading.

The place was packed, and not with its usual overabundance of sports fans, either, but instead with people who were looking forward to hearing Sergio read from *The Cumming of Christ*. These people were legitimate fans. They were a surreal sight. It was easy sometimes to think you were completely alone, talking to yourself, especially when your main source of communication and business was through the Internet. Seeing these people and hearing them talk about how pumped they were to listen to Sergio read reconfirmed what Nick had already expected: people loved the weird shit. They were just waiting for someone to give it to them. And thanks to Nick and his press, somebody was finally around to deliver the best weird shit available. BILF's readers were mostly underground, true, but that didn't mean the underground wasn't populated. It didn't mean there wasn't a global mosh pit going on under the world's feet. Who wanted to be aboveground, anyway?

Since they still had fifteen minutes, Sergio wanted to prepare for his reading. He ordered three shots of Jack. After he finished his drinks, he still had fourteen minutes to spare, so he spent the remainder of his time drinking more shots.

"Have you decided what you're going to read?" Stephen asked.

Sergio shrugged. "I don't think that matters."

"You gotta read something from *Christ*, man," Nick said. "That's what these people want. I mean, shit, look at that guy. He has a T-shirt of Jesus taking it in the ass."

"I never endorsed that shirt," Sergio said, smiling at it. "But man, I wish I had one."

"I'll contact some T-shirt printing places online," Nick said. "We'll see what we can do."

"Badass." He took another shot. "Oh, speaking of, I didn't bring the book with me. Does anybody have a copy?"

Nick, having anticipated this, pulled out a rolled-up copy from his back pocket and handed it to the author.

"Thanks." Sergio took the book and stared at the front for a moment, admiring its cover. The artist, Matthew Spooner, had really done a great job capturing Sergio's manic writing style. The cover, which featured Jesus Christ nailed to a cross made out of naked women, couldn't have been more perfect, especially Christ's orgasm face. It was glorious, it was holy, it was sexy. Nick also dug the Virgin Mary at the bottom of the cover, on her knees, giving Jesus a blowjob. He still couldn't believe that an English teacher had tried assigning this book to high school students. BILF really did have the craziest goddamn fans. But hey, it had certainly sparked some controversy, which followed with a crazy amount of book sales, even if it had resulted in that teacher's termination. Nick would send the poor guy some free books, maybe a boxset of Placid paperbacks.

A homeless man in a suit stumbled up to them, clearly drunk. "Hey, Nick, how's it goin', buddy?"

"Piss off, Jared."

"Whoa, whoa. Why so hostile?"

Nick just stared at him and waited for him to leave. Instead, the vagrant moved closer and said, "You know, in case you were looking to hire anybody to edit, I'm currently available."

"I know you're available. You're *always* available."

"Well, maybe you should hire me then."

"And maybe you should fuck off." Nick pushed him away and he got lost in the crowd of drunks. They had two minutes left until the reading began and the bar was becoming restless.

"Okay, troops, let's have another one," Sergio said. They ordered another round and tipped their glasses together before pouring them down their throats. "Okay," Sergio said, smiling at the burn, "it's time to go blow this universe a new asshole."

Sergio approached the stage with a copy of *The Cumming of Christ* over his head, and the crowd started going crazy. Sergio stood on top of the stage and looked down at the microphone, as if he'd never used one in his life, and shit, maybe he hadn't. None of them had ever attended a reading of this size before.

Sergio waved his hands up and down, signaling for the crowd to get louder, and they obeyed.

"Shit," Louise said. "This is insane."

"You think he's gonna write a follow-up?" Billy asked.

Nick nodded. "He's already written one."

"Shit, when?"

"Last week."

"That motherfucker's a robot, man."

"He's *my* robot," Nick said, smiling and taking another drink of his Shiner.

Sergio grinned wide and shouted into the microphone, "ARE YOU LOONY MOTHERFUCKERS READY TO GET CRAZY?"

The crowd shouted, "YES!"

"WHAT WAS THAT?"

"YES!"

"GIVE ME A FUCK YEAH."

"FUCK YEAH!"

"HAVE YOU SINFUL MOTHERFUCKERS ACCEPTED JESUS CHRIST AS YOUR LORD AND FUCK BUDDY?"

"FUCK YEAH!"

"HAVE YOU PREPARED YOURSELVES TO DO WHATEVER HE COMMANDS, WITHOUT QUESTION?"

"FUCK YEAH!"

"ARE YOU READY TO WORSHIP OUR LORD AND SAVIOR, JESUS CHRIST?"

"FUCK YEAH!"

"ARE YOU READY TO SWALLOW HIS HOLY CUM?"

"FUCK YEAH!"

Sergio took a moment to recover from laughing. "Okay, let's do this shit."

He opened up *The Cumming of Christ*. Stephen jumped up on the stage with his acoustic guitar and began ripping against the chords as loud as he could manage, and Sergio started screaming the words from a random page in his book.

"'JESUS CHRIST DON'T NEED NO MOTHERFUCKING FLUFFER!' JESUS SCREAMED, SLAPPING THE PORN STAR WITH HIS HOLY DONG."

The crowd evolved into a mosh pit. They screamed the passages along with Sergio, like they knew the book by heart.

"Oh my god," Billy said.

"Where have these people been hiding?" Louise asked, and Nick wondered if maybe she was feeling a little jealous that *Grits & Clits* wasn't as popular.

Sergio jumped up and down, kicking his legs in the air, acting like a true rock star. "'WATER AIN'T THE ONLY THING I CAN TURN INTO WINE, BITCH!' JESUS

SHOUTED IN GLEE AS SARAH PALIN DEEPTHROATED HER LORD AND SAVIOR."

Nick turned to Billy and shouted for him to go retrieve the promotional materials from the trunk.

"*What?*" Billy screamed back.

"THE PROMOTIONAL MATERIALS. GO GET THEM."

"WHAT PROMOTIONAL MATERIALS?"

"THE GODDAMN CRUCIFIXES."

Billy smiled. "Oh, yeah." He spun around and ran outside.

Nick noticed the bartender, pouring somebody a drink and shaking his head disapprovingly. He wore a crucifix necklace and a Bible verse tattooed across his throat. He made sure to be extra polite when he ordered another round of shots.

Billy returned with a box of promotional materials that Louise and Stephen had stayed up all night making. The design was simple enough. You just had to have the necessary supplies, which were lots of dildos and rolls of duct tape. Once you had those, you could make as many dildo crucifixes as your tiny perverted heart desired. At least until you ran out of dildos and duct tape.

Across the horizontal dildo on each crucifix, they had written "SERGIO PLACID'S THE CUMMING OF CHRIST" in black permanent marker. They'd used a red marker for the black crucifixes.

As Sergio's reading grew rowdier, Nick and his publishing staff began throwing the holy dildos into the massive mosh pit. The crowd eagerly snagged them out of the air, as if they were expecting them.

At the sight of dozens of drunken lunatics waving dildo crucifixes in the air, Sergio smiled wider and screamed louder.

"FIRST HE DIED FOR HER SINS, THEN HE JIZZED ON HER TITS."

The crowd exploded. They'd have to call in the riot

squad soon. Nick was loving it. He drank more beer, threw more dildo crucifixes.

Behind him, the bartender muttered, "You're all going to hell. Every last one of you."

Annoyed, Nick turned around to throw a dildo crucifix at him, only he threw his cell phone instead.

"That's it," the bartender said. "I'm calling the police."

"Call these nuts!" a random drunk screamed, and dropped his pants and proceeded to urinate over the bar.

Nick remembered laughing hysterically at the sight of the bartender dodging the stranger's piss, then somebody smacked Nick in the face with a dildo crucifix, and everything went blurry. He woke up the next morning covered in vomit.

Sitting in the parking lot now, Nick wondered who had to clean up the mess they left behind. Did the bartender have to stay late? Was he still there?

Was Nick really going to hell?

Only one way to find out. He got out of the car and approached the bar entrance.

The doors were locked.

"Balls."

12.
The Drive to Nowhere and Everywhere

"JESUS CHRIST, HOW long is this guy going to drive? Where could he possibly be taking us?"

"Forever. Anywhere."

"It just seems awfully long of a trip for someone he randomly recognized in a coffee shop."

"Maybe he'd been following me. Stalking me. Who knows."

"He could be taking us to the woods, where he has a grave already dug, waiting for you."

"Hopefully it's big enough to fit two bodies."

"That isn't funny."

"You're the one who keeps talking about it."

"What else do you expect me to talk about? The World Series?"

"Were you rooting for the Giants or the Royals?"

"Seriously?"

"You know, I was listening to this podcast a few days ago, the guest was this guy who writes junkie fiction. Joe Pitts or Tom Clifford, something like that. Anyway, he was watching game seven during the interview, and he went fucking berserk when the Giants won. It was pretty amazing."

HOW TO SUCCESSFULLY KIDNAP STRANGERS

"Are you not at all worried about where we're going?"

"Sure I am. But there's nothing I can do about it right now."

"We could come up with some sort of plan."

"A plan for what?"

"Uh. Freedom?"

"Listen, when they open this trunk, we could be facing an infinite amount of possibilities. We have no idea what's waiting for us. He could open the trunk and light us all on fire, or shit, he could never open the trunk at all, just drive off a cliff."

"I hadn't thought about that."

"See? Plans are useless."

"Shit."

"I gotta."

"What?"

"Shit. I gotta."

"Well. Please hold it."

"I'll try."

"Oh shit."

"I thought you wanted me to hold it."

"No, shut up, I think he's stopping."

"You're right."

"Oh shit."

10.
This Just In:
Everything Sucks

ELIZA MADE BILLY drive into a field, far from the road. Despite what her brother was telling her, and despite the pounding coming from the trunk, she still couldn't believe the situation. It was just too fucking crazy to be reality.

She told him to stay in the car and pop the trunk. She got out and walked around to the back of the car and waited. The trunk eventually popped open once Billy finally discovered the trunk release button in the front of the car. She slowly lifted it and peered inside. One man did not seem familiar at all, but the other guy she definitely knew.

Billy wasn't bullshitting. She'd recognize that smug asshole's face anywhere. Even if his face was now busted up and leaking a frightening amount of blood.

"Hi," the man she didn't recognize said.

"Hey," she said.

"What the fuck is going on?" Harlan Anderson said.

"Let me get back to you on that." Eliza closed the trunk and returned to the passenger seat.

"Well?" Billy said.

"Well what?"

"What are you thinking?"

Eliza laughed. She couldn't help it. "I think we're in way over our heads here."

"Shit. What else is new?"

"Maybe we should call Nick."

"I thought about that," Billy said, then frowned. "Except that I have Nick's cell."

"What? Why do you have his cell?"

"Last night, at the bar? Nick threw it at the bartender. Well, the bartender turned out to be a sweet ol' soul with a healthy supply of crank. He was the dude who took me to that party after the bar closed. He gave me Nick's cell, since he was holding on to it. He was thinking about pawning it, but decided I was a pretty okay guy, so gave it to me to give back to Nick."

"Okay," Eliza said. "Then I guess we can just go directly to his apartment."

"What if he's not home?"

"Nick is always home."

"You think Louise is home?" Billy smiled.

"You're a pervert."

"I am merely human, sis. Merely human."

"Barely human."

Eliza cringed, thinking about the last time they'd all partied together at Nick's apartment. Stephen passed out early, and Louise and Billy ended up fucking each other in the bathroom. Eliza heard all the details from her brother the next day, despite the fact that she'd plugged her ears and sung "la-la-la" to drown out his words. The fingers and singing didn't do an effective enough job and she still had to hear all about her brother's first anal sex experience (Louise being the penetrator and Billy being the penetrated, in this instance). Billy really needed more friends. Anyone, really, besides herself, who'd be willing to talk about sex with him.

They drove to Nick's apartment without further discussion. She didn't want to know what her brother was thinking. Sometimes people's thoughts were best left in their heads to die. Eliza's own mind was taking a turn for the worst. She should've just jumped out of the car and ran far away before shit continued downhill. But she didn't— of course she didn't. She had her chance back at the field, after looking into the trunk and seeing those men. She could have told them both to run and she could have fled with them. But she'd closed the trunk and gotten back in the car and told her brother to drive.

She was involved no matter what now, and as ugly as it sounded, this was her choice. Eliza had been given an exit opportunity and she'd willfully, stupidly ignored it.

Nick's apartment was unlocked, but nobody was inside. The bathroom was covered in vomit, which was typical for Nick's apartment. If someone wasn't puking, then the planet wasn't spinning.

Eliza and Billy sat on the torn sofa, staring at the nicotine-stained wall ahead of them.

"I really don't want to go to prison," Billy said.

"Well, you're probably going to," Eliza said, always the good sister.

"But now you're an accessory, yo."

"We'll figure something out."

"You think so?"

"Probably not."

Outside, somebody was mowing their lawn. Even nearer, right here in the apartment parking lot, two men were pounding on the inside of a trunk, begging for their lives to be spared. Eliza doubted anybody would pay the sound any attention. Nobody wanted to stumble across those kinds of horrors. It was easier to pretend you hadn't heard anything than to hear something and have to investigate.

Billy rubbed his hands through his hair. "I can't stay here in these conditions."

"Well, what do you want to do?"

"I need some roof time."

"What about me? What about your trunk buddies?"

"Sis, not now, okay?"

"Then when?"

"Goddammit, just calm down. Just . . . just . . . ugh, fuck."

Billy stood up and left the apartment before she could say anything else. She knew he was climbing the fire escape to the roof. He liked to go up there sometimes to get high. He probably had a stash hiding in one of the air vents.

Eliza sat on the sofa pondering the situation. They had two bodies in the trunk. Both of them alive, both conscious. Her brother had assaulted them. There was not going to be an easy way out of this, no matter how she tried to spin it.

There was another problem, of course. She couldn't just leave them in the trunk forever. She doubted there was much oxygen in there. Sometime soon, she'd need to figure out what to do. That, or they'd die, which might actually solve the problem.

Where was everybody, anyway? There was always someone here. The book reading last night must've been insane. She was glad she hadn't gone, though. She'd stayed home and completed a ton of work.

Goddamn. She didn't even recognize herself anymore.

Just a year ago, and she would've been the first person at the bar, licking LSD squares as she jerked-off the bartender for free shots. But she'd changed. At least, she'd tried to. She may have focused working more and partying less, but she was still somehow mixed up in a kidnapping situation. Hell, her life was more fucked-up than it ever had been.

14.
Jesus Fucking Christ

LOUISE AND STEPHEN pulled up in the parking lot, music blaring. Louise couldn't stop laughing and howling. "That was so fucking rad."

"We could have gotten arrested, Louise."

"I know!" She punched the glove compartment. "Oh God, I feel so alive."

Stephen shook his head, sweat dripping down his face. He tried to cut the engine, but Louise grabbed his hand and guided it between her legs, under her skirt.

"Let's fuck," she said.

"What, right here?"

She rolled her eyes. "Obviously. Come on. Let's do it right now."

Stephen laughed, then stopped when she didn't laugh with him. He looked around through the windows and shook his head. "No way. There's too many people here. The maintenance guy is right there mowing."

"So what?" She pushed his hand harder against her crotch. "Let's give him a show."

"Uh . . . " He closed his eyes and bit his tongue, lifting the edge of her panties up and rubbing her. A baby cried in a car nearby and he yanked his arm free. Ahead of them, they spotted Billy climbing up the apartment's fire escape. "I can't do this. I'm sorry. Let's just go inside where it's private."

"You pussy."

"I guess I am." He killed the engine and got out of the car. Halfway across the parking lot, they both froze, cappuccinos in hand, at the sound of something loud banging inside a car's trunk. It sounded like fists.

"Holy shit," Louise said, pressing her ear against the trunk. "I think someone's in here."

"Do you recognize this car?" Stephen asked.

"No. You?"

He shook his head.

"Help!" a voice shouted from inside the trunk. "Somebody please help us!"

Louise jumped back, gasping. "Shit, there really is someone in there." She leaned forward, over the trunk. "Hey! Whoever you are. Hold on a second. We'll bust you out."

She grabbed Stephen's hand and pulled him toward the apartment. "Where are we going?" he asked. "We need to call the police."

"Let's get the trunk opened first."

"How?"

"I don't know, maybe get like a knife and jimmy the lock or something."

"Would that work?"

"It happened in a movie once, so I guess it's possible."

They burst into Nick's apartment and discovered Eliza sitting on the sofa, crying. She screamed at their sudden entrance, which caused them both to scream, as well.

"What's wrong?" Eliza said.

"You won't believe this," Louise said, "but there's somebody locked in someone's trunk out there." She pointed behind her with her thumb.

"We gotta call the police," Stephen said.

Eliza jumped up and blocked Louise from progressing through the living room. "Uh, you may want to hold off on that."

Louise raised her brow, half-smiling. There was

something about the look in Eliza's eyes that told her everything she needed to know. Today was going to be one of the best days of her life. "And why should we hold off?" she asked, playing stupid.

And Eliza told them.

And Louise laughed long and hard until her stomach hurt. "Are you fucking serious, dude?"

Eliza nodded. "They're outside right now, locked in the trunk."

"Holy shitballs."

"Why the hell did you bring them to Nick's apartment?" Stephen asked, scratching the back of his head. "That wasn't the smartest idea."

"Oh shut the fuck up, party killer," Louise said. "This is awesome."

"Where *is* Nick, anyway?" Eliza scanned the living room again to reconfirm she hadn't overlooked his sleeping body.

Louise shrugged. "He was gone when we woke up."

"Dude probably went to Sergio's," Stephen said. "Who knows. Has anybody called him?"

"Billy has his phone. I guess Nick threw it at the bartender last night."

Louise nodded. "Yeah, that sounds about right." She paused. "Wait, what's stopping them from calling the police in the trunk? Don't they have phones?"

"Nah, Billy actually thought about that," Eliza said. "He took their phones and crushed them."

"How gangsta."

"All right, well, you guys gotta get out of here," Stephen said.

"Where are we supposed to go?" Eliza asked.

"You have an apartment. Take him there."

"But my apartment is on the sixth floor of my building, and the elevator is out. You guys are on the ground floor. Come on."

Stephen laughed. "Are you seriously suggesting bringing them in here?"

Eliza shrugged. "Sure, why not?"

"Absolutely not."

"Dude, this isn't even your apartment."

"And it's yours?"

Louise sighed and waved her hands up, a drop of her cappuccino splashing through the mouth hole. "Will everybody stop acting like a bunch of pussies? Let's just get these people out of the trunk before they fuckin' die in there."

They were quiet for a moment. Outside, the lawn mower continued its genocidal assault on grass.

"Okay," Stephen said. "How are we going to get them inside? They aren't tied up or anything, right? So we could open the trunk, but what stops them from jumping out and attacking us? What prevents them from running away?"

Louise set down her cappuccino and ran to the kitchen. She returned with a steak knife. "We could threaten them."

Eliza nodded. "Yeah, that'd work."

Stephen laughed, but more out of stress than humor. "I'm dating a wannabe psychopath."

"I don't understand the problem," Louise said.

"How many knives do we have?" Eliza asked. "You can't stab two people at once."

Louise laughed. "Kind of like knocking out two birds with one stone. Two hostages with one dull steak knife."

Eliza just stared at her.

"You know what would really work, though?" Louise smiled. "A gun."

"Nobody has a fucking gun, Louise," Stephen said. "Jesus fucking Christ. We operate a small press, not a fucking hitman-for-hire business."

Louise's face lit up and she pointed at him, excited. "That's it!"

"What's it?"

"You beautiful genius!" she said, and rushed to the back room. She returned with a leftover promo crucifix from *The Cumming of Christ*. One of the black ones.

"What are you gonna do with that?" Stephen asked. "Stimulate them until they cooperate?"

"No, asshole." Louise held the dildo crucifix close to her side, shielding the majority of the object with the sleeve of her jacket, letting only the head stick out. "Jesus fucking Christ indeed!"

"Uh."

"It looks like a gun, doesn't it?"

Stephen laughed. "No, not at all."

Eliza nodded. "I dig it."

Louise looked down at the mattress across the room. "What if we threw some pillowcases over their heads when we lead them in? That way they can't really see anything."

"I don't know," Stephen said. "I think it would look like we were about to execute them. People might freak out." He brushed the blinds aside and peeked through the window. "The maintenance guy is out there on his riding lawnmower. He'll see us."

"That guy sold me pot last week. I doubt he gives a shit," Louise said.

"This is a little more serious than selling pot."

"Ah, fuck this," Louise said, and stomped out of the apartment. Eliza and Stephen stayed behind a moment, giving each other a confused look, then followed her outside. She'd already found the trunk release button and popped it open and was dragging one of the hostages out and dropping him onto the cement. She held the dildo crucifix at her side and aimed it at the other guy in the trunk.

"Get the fuck out of the trunk, don't think I won't explode your faces with bullets, 'cause I totally will."

"Holy shit," Stephen said.

The other guy scrambled out of the trunk, lifting his hands. "Please don't shoot."

Harlan Anderson slowly climbed to his feet, also holding his hands up.

"What the hell do you guys want?"

HOW TO SUCCESSFULLY KIDNAP STRANGERS

"We want you to turn around and walk into the building. Apartment number twenty-three. Move your asses."

"And if we refuse?" Harlan asked.

"Then . . . uh." Louise paused, thought for a moment. "Look, dude, just get in the fuckin' apartment before shit gets ugly."

Harlan sighed, then he and the other hostage turned around and moved toward the apartment entrance. Stephen stared at his girlfriend, holding the knife she'd given him. She was waving at the maintenance man, who waved back at them, as if telling them to have a good day. Stephen couldn't resist laughing. It was the laugh of a man losing his grasp with reality.

"What's so funny?" Louise asked.

"You sound like you're in a movie."

"Maybe I am."

"This ain't Hollywood, babe," Stephen said.

"You're right. This is much more fun."

15.

The Universe Fattens & We Can No Longer Support Its Weight

O**N THE WAY HOME**, Nick stopped at the coffee shop. He was still starving. His apartment was a lost cause. There weren't even enough sofa crumbs for the mice to survive on.

An eReader greeted him outside the coffee shop, abandoned on the sidewalk. He picked it up and inspected the screen. It wasn't cracked or damaged in any apparent way. What kind of maniac just leaves a perfectly fine eReader on the sidewalk? He turned it on and found himself looking at an e-copy of a book he'd recently published: *The Cumming of Christ* by Sergio Placid.

Nick stared at it for a long time, not sure how to react. He laid it back down on the sidewalk and slowly backed away, entering the coffee shop. He typically didn't frequent these kinds of places, as they were often occupied by writers trying to shove half-finished manuscripts down his throat. All the local unpublished authors knew Nick from various conventions, and they were all lining up to tell him about the Great American Tentacle Novel already written inside their heads, they just needed to sit down and type it out.

The barista smiled as he approached the counter. "Hey, Nick."

"Hi, Lucy."

He smiled back, although his mind was still on the eReader. If he didn't at least smile back to her there was a good chance she would poison his order. A few years ago, they'd gone out for a couple of weeks. She also wanted to be a writer. She'd showed her one of his short stories and he'd told her it still needed some work. He didn't know what she wanted him to say. He wasn't going to lie. She'd asked for his honest opinion, as a small press publisher. So he'd given it to her. The relationship ended with her slamming a rollerblade into his scrotum. He still had the scar.

"You hear from Billy today?"

"Nah," Nick said. "We all went out to Nightscapes last night. Sergio was doing a reading. We got separated, no idea what happened to him. Why?"

Lucy's smile widened, like she had a juicy secret to spill. "Well, he came in here earlier this morning."

"Okay, and?"

"He was tweaking big time."

"What else is new."

"He attacked somebody."

"What?"

The woman in line behind Nick cleared her throat loudly. They ignored her.

"He jumped this dude outside the shop. I don't know who he is. But he must've pissed Billy off because that guy was *vicious*."

"Whoa."

"But that ain't all."

"What do you mean?"

The woman behind them cleared her throat again,

dragging it out. Nick turned around and asked if she wanted a cough drop. She quieted down.

Lucy continued. "So, get this, okay? When Billy was beating on that dude, some *other* dude stopped his car to help, and Billy started kicking his ass, too."

"Jesus."

"I know, right?"

"I wonder what he was on."

"Well, he'd just bought a lemon pound cake."

"That'll do it."

"But, okay, get this crazy shit." Lucy leaned forward on the counter. He tried and failed not to glance at her cleavage. "When Billy finished beating them, he threw 'em both in the driver's trunk and drove off."

"What?"

"He straight up kidnapped them."

"Holy shit."

"I know! The cops were here and everything. One of them even asked for my number. Like, as if, right?"

"Did they catch Billy?"

"Not that I know of."

"Shit."

"I know. Where do you think he'd take them?"

Nick bit his lip. "Probably my place."

"Oh, yeah, that makes sense."

"What did you tell the cops?"

She shook her head. "Nothing. I said I didn't recognize either of them."

"What about the guy Billy jumped?"

"Nah, dude. I mean, he comes in sometimes and fucks around on his iPad or whatever, but I don't know him or anything."

"All right. Thanks. I'll find Billy, try to straighten this shit out."

"No problem." She thought for a moment, then said, "So, I've been working on this new story . . . "

"I'll have a scone, please."

16.
Kidnappers & Hostages

HARLAN AND HIS trunk companion were pushed into the apartment. The man who'd attacked them outside the coffee shop was mysteriously absent, which was fortunate. The man was a psychopath and every second they spent separated was a second Harlan could avoid breaking out into an anxiety attack. He looked around the apartment and grimaced. He didn't care if they *were* kidnappers. They could have at least tidied up a little before snatching him. "This place is a pigsty."

"Ah, it's not too bad," Lewis said. "It beats my trunk."

"Quit kissing the kidnappers' asses."

"Yeah," one of the women said, sipping from a gas station coffee cup. "We know this place is trashed. What's your name, anyway?"

"L-Lewis."

"Well, Lewis, you don't need to lie. We aren't going to let you go because of compliments."

"Well, what will make you let us go?"

"Hmm. We don't know yet."

The other woman, the one who'd opened the trunk an hour or so ago and looked at them, then freaked out and closed it again, sat at the edge of the couch, staring at her hands. Her body was shaking. Maybe she was in shock. He didn't know why she was acting like a victim. She wasn't the one fucking kidnapped. She wasn't the one who'd been attacked on the street and stuffed into a trunk. She wasn't the one who'd lost her eReader in the middle of the street. Some homeless person had probably found it by now and bartered it for crack cocaine.

"Why are we even here?" Harlan asked, almost in a growl. "Why did that asshole jump me? Do you guys think I have money? Because oh my god, that'd be hilarious."

"And, really," Lewis said, "there's no reason at all you'd want me. It's him you want. I have nothing to do with any of . . . whatever this is about."

Harlan sneered at him. "Dick."

Lewis exhaled. "This isn't my fight."

But Harlan was no longer paying listening to Lewis. His attention was stolen, refocused on the many stacks of books piled along the walls of the living room. Books everywhere. Books he recognized. Books he regularly reviewed on his blog.

"Why . . . why do you have so many BILF Publishing books?" He knelt down and traced his finger along the cover of Nick Twig's *The Trampoline Incident*. Possibly one of the worst books he'd ever read in his life. Talk about pretentious trash.

"What's a BILF?" Lewis asked.

"It stands for 'Books I'd Like to Fuck'," the male kidnapper said.

"That's, uh . . . that's an interesting name."

Harlan still couldn't process what he was seeing. "But, why . . . ?"

The women drinking coffee set the cup down and stepped forward, smiling and lifting her arm up and revealing the true identity of the dildo crucifix. "SERGIO PLACID'S THE CUMMING OF CHRIST" could clearly be read across the horizontal sex toy.

Harlan gasped and stepped back, dropping *The Trampoline Incident*. "No . . ."

She nodded. "Yes."

He turned to the other hostage, the one named Lewis. "Run! These people are going to fucking kill us! *Help! HELP!*"

Harlan sprinted toward the door.

Behind him, the woman who'd been drinking coffee shouted, "Halt!" Then something bashed into the back of his skull and he fell forward, slamming his face into the bottom of the door. He turned around and sat against the door, holding the dildo crucifix in his lap. He thought he saw a drop of his blood on one of its tips. The fucking thing was deadly.

Lewis looked at Harlan, then at the steak knife in the male kidnapper's hand, and opted to sit down on the couch. "I think the apartment is perfectly fine."

"Take off your belt," the dildo crucifix thrower said.

The male kidnapper cleared his throat. "What the fuck, Louise?"

She rolled her eyes. "Shut up, doofus." She nodded at Lewis. "Come on, off with it." She looked down at Harlan, still groaning on the floor. "You too, dickwad."

Louise and Eliza tied the hostages' arms behind their backs while Stephen paced around the living room. Once in a while he'd look at the knife in his hand and gasp, then continue pacing.

A car started up. Stephen stepped outside just in time to see Lewis's vehicle speed out of the parking lot. "I think Billy just took off."

"Of course he did," Eliza said, still on the couch next to Lewis. She had managed to finally stop shaking, but her skin was still pale and sickly. "Like he'd ever clean up one of his own messes."

"Can somebody please explain why this is happening?" Lewis asked. "I'm so confused."

"Sure," Harlan said, looking more pissed off than

afraid. "These psychopaths run a small press. They publish these weird little bizarro books. And, on my book review blog, I've given some negative criticism of some of their books. And now, I guess, they must want some kind of revenge, because god forbid they ever actually learn how to write." He looked at Louise. "That about sum it up?"

Louise looked at him for a minute, giving him the same kind of look a parent might give her misbehaving child. "You said *Grits & Clits* was the product of a mentally challenged child molester eating crayons and shitting out words."

"Whoa," Lewis said. "That's harsh."

Louise nodded. "Right?"

Harlan shrugged. "I stand by what I said."

"Wow," Eliza said. "What a complete dick."

"Yeah," Stephen said. "No wonder your brother kidnapped him. Jesus Christ."

"Hmm," Harlan said. "You said our attacker's name was Billy, right? I'm guessing he's the one responsible for that *Chlamydia Kamikaze* book." He looked at Eliza. "And if you're his sister, that must make you Eliza. The so-called 'interior designer'. No wonder the insides of the books look so shitty."

"Fuck you."

He nodded to Louise. "And you're obviously Louise Truesdale." He looked to Stephen. "And you must be our wonderful editor-in-chief, Mr. Nick Twig."

"No, I'm Stephen, man."

"Who?"

"I, uh, do photography sometimes."

"Then where's your loyal commander? Where is Nick?"

17.
Ugh

OFFICER JOSEPH NOUS was having a bad day. Twice in a row he'd been called to an assault-in-progress, and both times the perpetrators got away. The second time, he walked past them, even *talked* to them, and still let them continue on their way. Then he tried to arrest the man who'd been assaulted, the big biker guy. That hadn't gone over too well. The biker was threatening to sue the police department now. Joseph was dreading his inevitable return to the station. His captain was going to kick his ass. And maybe he deserved it. Only a moron would let two criminals stroll right past him.

He was ready to go home. He wanted to snuggle with his wiener dog and forget about all his many, many inadequacies. Unfortunately, his shift wasn't close to over. It'd never be over. Even in death, he'd have to wear this stupid uniform. He'd have to walk around with this pointless badge. Have to carry a gun he knew he would never use, not even if it meant saving someone's life. He was a coward. An idiot. He knew it and so did everybody else.

He headed for his speeding-trap, thinking he'd had enough bullshit for one day. He was just going to read *The Cumming of Christ* and relax. If someone wanted to speed past him, then screw it, let them speed. He wasn't going after anyone else today. If the mafia executed the Governor in front of his squad car, he wouldn't look up from his book. He was officially done.

First a kidnapping, and now a gas station brawl? Who kidnaps people anymore? Who fights in gas stations? The whole world was inhabited by savages. And it was supposed to be his job to protect them? How could you protect something that wanted so desperate to destroy itself? You couldn't. *He* couldn't. He wouldn't. In high school, he was so nervous he shit his pants during his graduation speech. How could he be expected to stop a kidnapper?

According to dispatch, nobody had a clue who this kidnapper was, anyway, nor the man he attacked in front of the coffee shop. They had video surveillance of their faces, and the news was currently broadcasting the images on TV, so hopefully that would lead to someone recognizing one of them.

But at least they knew the identity of the man who'd been driving the car and stopped to help, thanks to an outside camera being able to read the license plate numbers. The car belonged to a Mrs. Helga Hill, who had been murdered two days ago in her home. The primary suspect was her currently missing husband, Lewis Hill.

18.

The Superman of Christians Loves Math

THE PUBLISHING COMPANY duct taped the hostages' mouths and dragged them into the closet. It was their best temporary solution. Maybe it could be their permanent solution. Just leave them in there until they eventually suffocated or starved to death. Buy a bunch of nice smelling candles to block out the scent of decay. Eventually they would just be bones, and they could use them as Halloween decorations. Win-win.

Louise brought up this option to the others, but they didn't seem to be on board. Bummer.

"All right, then what's your brilliant plan?" she asked, leaning back in the kitchen chair. They were all at the table, drinking shitty coffee from unwashed mugs they'd stolen from Denny's months ago. It was a drastic downgrade from the gas station cappuccino. The kitchen was typically used for business meetings. Today it was being used to debate kidnapper etiquette.

"I just don't get why Billy would do this in the first place," Stephen said. "I mean, yeah, he's been a dick online and stuff, but holy shit, kidnapping? This is way over our heads. We're all going to prison."

"He was high as hell this morning," Eliza said. "Wasn't

in his right mind at all. He'd said he'd been up all night, doing meth with some bartender."

Louise laughed. "The one from Nightscapes?"

"Yeah, I think so."

"That dude was ultra-Christian. Like, the Superman of Christians."

"Well, the Superman of Christians loves meth, apparently."

Louise laughed and drank coffee. Stephen sat still, his coffee long cold and untouched, pale.

"Whatever Billy did, it's already done," Eliza said. "And whether we like it or not, we are definitely involved."

"I am not involved in any of this," Stephen said.

"Dude, you waved a knife at them," Louise said. "Not to mention the fact we just robbed a gas station this morning. Why not add another offense to our beautiful, growing list?"

"Good point."

"Wait, what?" Eliza said.

Louise shrugged. "Just a little assault and robbery this morning. No big deal."

Stephen raised his hand. "Uh, it was totally a big deal. What are you talking about?"

Louise dismissed him with an eye-roll. "I'm telling you guys. Let them rot for eternity in the closet."

Stephen gulped. "That's not even funny."

"What if we let them go?" Eliza asked. "Right now, just untie them, and walk 'em out the front door? Do you think they'd rat us out?"

Louise shook her head. "I don't know about the one dude, but that Harlan motherfucker most definitely would. You've read his reviews. Fuck him."

"Well, if we can't let them go, then . . . what are we going to do?"

Hands trembling, Stephen said, "Maybe we could bribe them."

Louise laughed. "Bribe them with what? We run a small press. None of us have any money."

"Oh, yeah."

"Maybe Eliza could fuck them in exchange for their silence," Louise suggested.

"Fuck you," Eliza said.

"No, not me. Fuck *them*."

"Who are we fucking?" Nick asked, standing in the walkway between the living room and kitchen.

Everybody at the table jumped at the sound of his voice, then settled down when they realized it was only their faithful editor-in-chief and not the police.

"Oh my god," Stephen said. "I almost just had a heart attack."

"How long have you been here?" Eliza asked.

"Just walked in." Nick took a bite of a scone.

Louise smiled, genuinely excited. "Wait until you find out what kind of fucking crazy shit you've missed."

Nick nodded. "I have one question, first."

"But wait, you—"

"Where are the people Billy kidnapped?"

The table was quiet for a moment, until Eliza asked, "Where have you been?"

Nick held up the half-eaten scone. "Coffee shop."

19.
That's What She Said

THEY DRANK MORE shitty coffee and thought about the situation. Billy was still missing in action. Nick wondered if he'd ever see him again. If he did, he was pretty sure he'd punch him in the face.

If it wasn't for Eliza, Billy wouldn't even be involved with the company. The guy wrote one book and it sucked, but Nick still published it, because the press needed Eliza's formatting skills. She was cheap and local, plus she was a friend. Going with somebody else would be a disaster, so yeah, he published Billy's novella, *Attack of the Chlamydia Kamikazes,* and a year later it still hadn't received a single sale on Amazon—except for the one Billy's mom was pressured into purchasing. Yet he acted like he was this big bad author, doing whatever the fuck he pleased. Like kidnapping reviewers, for instance. Sure, a reviewer who was a complete asshole and probably deserved a good kidnapping, but still, Nick had to clean up the mess.

Harlan Anderson. He'd been a pain in Nick's ass for four years now, since he started up Books I'd Like to Fuck. Harlan had been one of the original writers to submit a manuscript during BILF's first month of open submissions. Harlan had also been the first writer Nick declined.

He still remembered Harlan's novel submission. He

was reminded of it every time Harlan wrote some shit about the press on his stupid blog. Harlan's novel, *That's What She Said*, was perhaps the dumbest goddamn book Nick had ever read. It was basically fifty thousand words written in free verse, one line with a planted innuendo and the following line always being, "THAT'S WHAT SHE SAID!". It went on like that for fifty thousand motherfucking words. Like if scientists tried to create a spambot based off the mind of Michael Scott from *The Office*. Since then, Nick had published some definitely strange shit, but nothing as pitiful as Harlan Anderson's self-proclaimed magnum opus.

Admittedly, the rejection letter had been a bit harsh, but this was back before Nick had any idea what the hell he was doing. It was his original intention to respond to every single manuscript with a long, personalized rejection. He never meant to be mean, but he was an asshole by nature. What kind of human being suggests to another human being they should toss their keyboard into the ocean?

In any case, that rejection had marked Harlan as an enemy for life. Once Nick began publishing actual titles, Harlan would somehow review them all—which he openly admitted to illegally downloading—and not once had he said anything positive.

The first book Harlan had reviewed was Nick's own novel, *The Trampoline Incident*. Harlan bashed him for publishing his own writing under his publishing company, calling Nick a piece of shit two-bit criminal who couldn't cut it with normal writers, so he had to hide behind a faux company he invented. It had definitely hurt Nick, as it was the first review he'd ever received for any of his writing, anywhere. Maybe some of it hit home. Maybe Harlan had a point. But then the review ended with Harlan suggesting Nick toss his keyboard into the ocean, and he finally realized who this guy really was, and that anything he said was just bitter resentment, so fuck him.

And fuck him again for making Nick feel guilty for the kidnapping. The asshole should have known words have consequences. Sure, these consequences were a bit extreme, but this was reality—*everything* was extreme.

Nick wheeled his huge classroom-sized whiteboard into the kitchen. The majority of the board was occupied with sloppy, schizophrenic scribblings of publication schedules, marketing plans, and upcoming local book festivals. Nick erased a grocery list at the top right corner and wrote, in big capital letters: **KIDNAPPING PLAN**.

"Okay," he said, pacing in front of the board, "the way I see it, we only have a few options here. Because let's face it, we are now kidnappers. All of us."

Stephen groaned. Louise smiled.

"The moment we allowed Billy to bring those two into this apartment, we became accessories. This makes us just as involved as he is."

"So, what're our options?" Eliza asked.

"Okay, so, we could just let them go," Nick said. "Maybe they won't say anything to the police, but they probably will."

On the board, he wrote: **RELEASE THE HOSTAGES**.

"Or we could bribe them into not talking, except none of us have any money."

BRIBERY.

"Or, another option, we never let them go. We keep them forever, as our prisoners."

LIFETIME IMPRISONMENT.

"Holy shit, that's fucked up," Eliza said.

Stephen buried his face in his hands.

Louise sat up straight. "I already suggested that, but nobody was down, man. I even thought we could use their bones as Halloween decorations. Smart, right?"

Nick nodded, knowing how insane they all sounded and not knowing what to do about it. Some days were crazier than other days, and today was definitely an 'everything is batshit' kind of day. Half of him felt like he was still asleep. None of this was real. His body moved on autopilot while his mind drifted to the clouds.

"I don't know," Nick said. "Maybe we could take them to Sergio's uncle's cabin. Hell. There is a vast amount of problems with that option, obviously."

"And the other options?" Eliza asked.

"Well." Nick paused a moment, not believing what he was about to say. "We could kill them."

On the board, he wrote: **MURDER.**

Stephen vomited all over the table. Everybody screamed.

20.
Heads Are Gonna Roll

LEWIS HADN'T INTENDED to murder his wife. Sure, he'd killed people in the past, no problem, but his wife was never supposed to become a victim. In fact, he loved his wife. She was the most beautiful woman on the planet. He would have done anything for her. But then she discovered the videos he'd saved on his laptop, and after that she found the severed heads in the basement, so yeah, obviously she had to go. He loved her but he wasn't fucking *crazy*.

If he hadn't come home from work early that day, he would probably be in prison right now. Helga would have undoubtedly called the police, if she'd been given a chance. But fate had other plans. Work ended early that day due to some bogus Ebola scare tactics puked out by the media, so Lewis drove home, thinking he'd surprise his wife in bed, make love to her, then take her out for a nice meal. Except when he came home, he couldn't find her. He looked everywhere. She was gone. He went into his office—despite the fact that she knew she wasn't allowed in there—and of course he didn't find her. But he did notice his laptop was powered on, and on the screen played one of his homemade snuff films.

He froze. As fast as a tree branch snapping, everything was ruined. The life he'd worked so hard to build was destroyed. Now he'd have to leave, get as far away as he could, and make a new life. He'd always expected this would happen, but not so soon. He needed more time to plan, more time to spend with his wife, whom he loved.

She wasn't supposed to die yet. She was never supposed to die.

He found her in the basement. She was going through the deep freezer he stored his deer meat in. All the deer meat was now on the floor, and she was standing above the freezer, staring at its other contents.

The heads.

Lewis thought about saying something, thought about apologizing. But it would have only made what he had to do that much more difficult. His life was already difficult enough, thank you.

He calmly tiptoed down the basement steps, walked up to his wife, and slit her throat. When the life had drained out of her and the tears had drained out of him, he collected one of his saws and proceeded to add a new, unexpected addition to his collection.

Before he left, Lewis stored his heads in a duffle bag and hid the bag in the trunk of his car. He didn't know how much distance he could gain before someone discovered his wife's headless corpse, but he was willing to bet he'd at least make it across state lines, if not farther. His wife wasn't exactly the most social type, plus she was unemployed, so there was no real reason to panic just yet. The only flaw in this plan was Helga's obnoxious bitch of a mother, who talked to her on the phone at least once a day. After a few days of not answering her calls, she'd either send someone to the house or fly down herself. Then the shit would hit the fan.

Hopefully, Lewis would be in Mexico by then.

Of course, he hadn't expected this slight kidnapping detour. This had definitely thrown him off his itinerary. He'd been driving for over two days and had only stopped to fall asleep in truck stop parking lots. He hadn't eaten since he left home. His body was overheated, rotting, dying. So he got off the highway, thinking he'd stop for a burger or something. He doubted the police were after him yet. Helga's headless corpse was still at home, being feasted on by insects. Only instead of a burger, he stumbled across some lunatic beating the shit out of another guy. In all honesty, he probably wouldn't have even stopped if they hadn't been right in the middle of the road. The burger joint was in sight, but he couldn't fit his car around them, so he was left without a choice. He got out and grabbed the psycho off the other guy, thinking how good it'd feel to decapitate the both of them. Except it didn't come to that. The man had some kind of superhuman strength. Maybe it was drugs. Maybe it was insanity. Lewis understood insanity. Insanity fueled humanity. In any case, Lewis was quickly overpowered, and soon he was on the ground next to the other guy, getting his face punched in.

He kind of found it funny. This is what happened when you tried to be nice, when you tried to help someone else out. You got the shit kicked out of you. You got kidnapped.

Ah well. It wasn't that big of a deal. These dumbasses clearly had no idea what they were doing. It was only a matter of time before they slipped up, and then he'd be back on his way to Mexico, his collection in the trunk a little heavier.

21.
Halloween Decorations

"**SO, LET'S SAY** we kill them," Nick said, already knowing it would never come to that. He'd rather go to prison than have to resort to murder, or allow any of his friends the same fate. Except maybe Billy. That fucker. Wherever he was hiding. But still, it was a fair option, and Nick felt he ought to let the fantasy play out so they could move on to serious ideas.

"How would we do it?" Louise asked.

Nick didn't have an answer for that question, and after a few minutes of disturbing silence, nobody else did either. He sighed, relieved. He really didn't want anybody to already have a murder plan. He didn't doubt for a second that they could come up with some creative ways to kill and dispose of the hostages, but none of them were about to seriously consider the possibility. They were writers, not killers.

When Nick moved on to the next option, Stephen's face returned to a somewhat normal color. It was clear he'd been on the verge of puking again, and everybody was relieved when it didn't happen.

"Right, so we won't kill them," Nick said. "And, no offense, guys, but I highly doubt we're capable of taking care of two grown men for the rest of our lives without anybody catching us, so that option is out, too. Which leaves us with just letting them go."

"Should we ask for a ransom first?" Louise asked, and Stephen shook his head, disgusted. "What? How the fuck else are we ever gonna make bank if we don't cash in on a couple of opportune hostages, right?"

"You're crazy," Stephen said. "I can't do this anymore with you."

"Whatever, dude."

Nick cleared his throat. He didn't have time for their petty shit. "A ransom would draw more attention to the police, don't you think? We don't really want that. The less attention, the better."

"Is that true, though?" She leaned forward, excited again. "Think about it, guys. We could be fuckin' famous. Screw this being poor, hustling bullshit. No more panhandling online for people to buy our books. We could be famous. Go on the run, rob some places, kidnap more people. We'd be motherfuckin' legends."

Stephen pushed back from the kitchen table and stood up. "Fuck this."

"Sit down, man," Nick said, irritated. He looked at Louise. "Maybe you're game for the life on the run fate, but not all of us are quite ready."

Eliza nodded. "Sorry, Louise. But I'd rather continue staying home all day in my pajamas, watching Netflix."

Louise rolled her eyes. "Okay, whatever. But just so you all know?" She pointed at Stephen. "This motherfucker and I held up a gas station before any of this kidnapping shit started. If we were alone, he'd totally be into this."

"I would not. This isn't who I am. And this isn't who *you* are."

"Whatever." She lit a cigarette and nodded at Nick. "Continue, I *guess*."

Nick waited for Stephen to sit back down, then he went on. "So, what we have to ask ourselves is this: if we let these people go, apologize, tell them Billy was high and didn't know what he was doing, do we think they will be cool? Or will they run straight to the police?"

"Considering we've beaten them up a little, tied them up, and locked them in the closet, I'm thinking they won't be so chill about the whole situation," Eliza said.

"Maybe we should just ask them," Stephen said.

Louise snorted. "Yeah, like they won't say whatever we want to hear to get us to let them go. What's to stop them from running to the pig-pen once they're out the door?"

Stephen settled back in his chair, pale again. "Yeah, I guess we can't really take them on their word."

"Especially Harlan," Nick said. "I don't know about the other one. I haven't talked to him, but you guys have. How is he?"

"I think he said his name was Lewis. He's all right," Eliza said. "If we let him go, he'd probably just get in his car and drive home, grateful we didn't kill him or whatever."

"Do you guys not watch any *Law and Order*?" Louise asked, looking at them like they were all pitiful losers. "Billy stole that guy's car in front of a public, crowded area. Places with cameras. Don't you think the police have already recovered the license plate of the car and have obtained this dude's identity? He goes home, they're gonna be waiting for him, with lots and lots of questions. And he isn't just gonna stay quiet. Not for nothin'."

"What are you suggesting?" Nick asked.

"I was right," Stephen said, trying to smile and failing. "We have to bribe them."

Eliza nodded. "It makes sense to me. Give them something for their troubles, make all this fucked-up shit worth it."

"None of us have any money, though," Louise said. "I feel like we've been through this. I'm telling you guys, they would make sweet Halloween decorations."

Eliza looked up at Nick, standing by his whiteboard. "What do we have in the publishing account?"

Embarrassed, he shrugged. "I don't know, not much, if anything at all. I just paid royalties last week, so the account is pretty much wiped out."

"Anything in the Paypal?"

"Maybe like twenty bucks, I don't know. I'd have to check."

"Twenty dollars isn't going to mean shit to these two," Louise said. "It'd be like pissing in their faces. Oh, *hey*, we could always piss in their faces."

Eliza made a screwed-up face. "Why are you always trying to piss on people?"

Louise shrugged. "Some people like it."

"Who would possibly like that?"

"Well—"

Stephen pounded his fist on the kitchen table. "Louise, shut up."

Louise started laughing. Eliza looked at Stephen, then quickly turned away.

"All right." Nick rubbed his eyes, already exhausted. Nobody plans on waking up to a hostage negotiation. "So, let's say we try to bribe them for their silence. How much do you think it's going to take?"

They all shrugged. Nick tossed his whiteboard marker in the sink and ran his hands through his hair.

"Fuck. Why is this so hard?"

"Why don't we just ask them?" Stephen said.

"What?"

"Let's just open the closet and ask them what it'll take."

"What if they say they don't want anything?" Nick said.

"Then we'll know they're lying," Louise said.

22.
Big Bang Theory T-Shirt Wearing Motherfucker

HARLAN SPENT THE majority of his time in the closet trying to decide if the staff of BILF Publishing was capable of murder. He knew that's what they were all talking about in the other room, but even when he pressed his head against the closet door, he still couldn't make out what they were saying.

He settled back into the darkness against Lewis, who hadn't moved since being shoved in here. Harlan wondered if he was even awake—or, for that matter, alive.

And if he was alive, Harlan didn't suspect Lewis would be of much help. The man had pretty much fed Harlan to the sharks before they'd been tied up. He couldn't trust the man. It was up to Harlan and Harlan only to escape.

He could barely hear the publishing company talking in the other room, but he got the feeling they were debating ways to dispose of his body. How fucking ridiculous. All he'd done was write some negative reviews. He did not deserve this. Writers weren't supposed to respond to criticism. They were supposed to read it, cry a little, and move on. But kidnapping? Totally unprofessional. What a bunch of crybabies.

If someone had asked him yesterday whether he

thought the brilliant minds behind BILF Publishing were crazy enough to murder another human being over a review, Harlan would have laughed. Now, though, he wasn't sure. These nutjobs obviously had no idea what they were doing. The tweaker had acted in the spur of the moment. None of this was planned.

This kidnapping had been dumped on everybody else's lap. They hadn't anticipated any of this shit when they woke up today, yet here he was, tied up in a closet. They had to be freaking out right now. He knew what they were thinking: the easiest solution right now would be to kill the hostages, dump the bodies, and pray nobody traced the crime back to them. That's what he would be thinking, at least, if the tables were turned. There was no way in hell Harlan would let *his* hostages go.

When you were afraid, you were easily convinced. And these assholes were terrified. If one person suggested turning the hostages into corpses, it wouldn't take much for the rest to agree.

Harlan wondered if anybody was looking for him. The coffee shop fight had plenty of witnesses, people standing around watching and taking photos and being generally unhelpful. But he didn't know any of those people, and they didn't know him. The police were trying to find a friendless man. A man without any real family, a man who lived alone and spent his free time reading shitty eBooks and warning others not to waste their money.

Maybe next week, when he didn't turn up for work, somebody would show some concern. Concern not for his health, of course, but for who was going to cover his shift.

But what about his closet-buddy, Lewis? Harlan didn't know much about him, despite being locked in various prisons together for the majority of the day. He probably had some sort of family. They'd be worried sooner than Harlan's boss. Hell, they probably already called the cops. Plus, there had to be security cameras somewhere in the shopping center close to the coffee shop. He wondered if footage had captured Lewis's license plates. Maybe the police were tracking down his stolen car. Would they think to look . . . wherever they were? Some apartment building, that was obvious, but beyond that, Harlan didn't know. When he was pulled out of the trunk, he tried to give the area a look-around, but he didn't recognize any of it. Just buildings and cars, the same as any other shit-for-nothin' town. Maybe someone at the coffee shop had recognized the tweaker who'd nabbed them. Maybe rescue was only minutes away. Or maybe these assholes would scare themselves into killing him, and that would be it—he'd be dead, over a bunch of stupid reviews.

It would be a fitting conclusion to an admittedly pathetic life.

His kidnappers' voices grew closer, and he realized they were approaching the closet just before the door opened and he came tumbling out, landing on the living room carpet. Lewis landed on top of him, knocking the wind out of him a second time. If his mouth wasn't duct taped, he would have shouted, "Fuck!" Instead, he shouted, "Ffuufff!"

A man he hadn't seen before but immediately recognized as Nick Twig turned both of them over and pulled the tape off their mouths. He stayed there a moment, crouched over them, staring into Harlan's eyes.

"Harlan," he said.

"Nick," Harlan said.

"It's about time we finally met."

Harlan nodded. "It's been a long time coming."

Nick looked to the other male—Stephen?—and gestured at the ground. "Help me get these two up to the couch."

"Why me?" Stephen asked.

"Because I asked you to. Come on."

Hesitant, Stephen picked up Lewis by his shoulders and dragged him to the couch, plopping him down into a sitting position on the cushion. Nick grabbed Harlan and did the same, then sat down on a fold-up chair in front of them, switching his gaze from Harlan to Lewis, Lewis to Harlan.

"So, how are you doing?" Nick asked.

Harlan laughed.

"Pretty thirsty," Lewis said. "I'd love a Pepsi."

Nick looked at him, like he forgot he was even here. "Would water be all right?"

"Is it bottled?"

"Nah."

Lewis scoffed. "Never mind."

Nick laughed. "Sorry, man. Not exactly rich. Sometimes you have to have to weigh your options: do you want to spend your last couple bucks on Pepsi, or beer? Well, we usually choose beer."

"I wouldn't mind a beer."

"We don't have any beer."

Lewis fell quiet.

Harlan glanced around the living room at the other psychos who'd kidnapped them. They all seemed nervous and refused to look him directly in the eyes, like they were dogs embarrassed of their own shit. He looked back at Nick, the only one who seemed to have enough courage to face the situation.

"So," Harlan said, "how are you going to kill us?"

The man behind them, Stephen, squealed. Nick didn't seem fazed, though. He just slowly shook his head and said, "Probably in some inadequate way you'll find disappointing, I'm sure."

"Passive-aggressive, much?"

"An asshole, much?" Nick asked.

Harlan nodded. "You've read my blog. Do you really have to ask that question?"

Nick smirked. "I've also read your novel."

"You fuck."

One of the girls—Harlan couldn't remember who was who—stepped forward. "Uh, Nick? Maybe this isn't the best time to start an argument."

HOW TO SUCCESSFULLY KIDNAP STRANGERS

Nick stared at him, fuming. If Harlan wasn't tied up, he might've punched him. It was a punch that'd been due for a long time now.

The girl wedged herself between them and kneeled down until she was eye-level with Harlan. "Hi, my name's Eliza."

"The formatter."

She tried to smile. "Yeah, that's right, the formatter."

Harlan never expected someone involved in BILF Publishing to be so attractive. He lost his voice for a moment. He'd talked to her earlier, but he'd been too full of rage to really give a shit about anything besides yelling at everybody. "Well, congratulations, the formatting is about the only decent praise I can give to your guys' books. Although that isn't really saying much."

He could hear Nick cursing under his breath behind her, and it made him laugh.

Eliza ignored the comment. "Listen, you realize we didn't intend for any of this to happen, right? My brother, the one who attacked you? He has a drug problem. I'm really sorry for all this. He didn't mean you any harm. When this happened, he wasn't in a right state of mind."

"Your brother should be put down."

"Maybe he should," Eliza said. "But right now, we need to discuss what's going to happen between us, don't you think?"

"I think it's pretty obvious what you're going to do," Harlan said, sighing and leaning back on the couch. "You're going to kill us."

Behind them, the other woman—*Louise?*—shouted, "Gonna turn your asses into Halloween decorations!"

Harlan didn't know what that meant and he didn't want to find out.

Lewis snorted. Eliza looked at Nick, unsure, then back at Harlan. "Why would you think that?"

"Quit bullshitting us. The only way out of this is by dumping our bodies in a lake, or something. You know it just as well as I do."

"What if we just let you go?" she asked.

"I would be okay with that," Lewis said. "I vote for this plan."

Harlan shook his head. Surely they'd already thought this out. "If you let us go, what's stopping us from going to the police?"

Eliza shrugged. "Nothing, I suppose. But maybe we can cheer you up a bit before letting you go, then, hmm, I don't know, you might not even care that we ruined your day."

Harlan leaned forward, intrigued. "And how exactly are you going to cheer me up?"

"I would be plenty content with just being let go," Lewis said. "Seriously."

"No you wouldn't," Harlan said. "Shut up."

"We were thinking some type of monetary compensation for your troubles," Eliza said.

Harlan laughed. "If you guys had cash, then your marketing strategy wouldn't boil down to begging people to buy your books on Facebook."

"You piece of shit, *Big Bang Theory* T-shirt-wearing motherfucker," Nick said, pushing Eliza out of the way. "Louise was right. Let's just kill them."

He tried to grab Harlan, but Eliza pulled him away before he could successfully wrap his hands around his throat.

"Okay, look," Eliza said. "Enough with this being-an-asshole shit, from the both of you. I'm trying to solve this issue, and neither of you seem like you want it solved."

"Sorry," Nick said.

"Sorry," Harlan said.

"So, Harlan, how much is it going to take to make up for what we've done to you today?" She looked at Lewis. "You, too."

Lewis shrugged. "I don't know, you guys don't have to pay us anything."

"Yes, we do."

"Hmm. Twenty-five bucks? Forty? I guess I would

definitely appreciate it if you can fill up my gas tank, since y'all have been driving my car around all day."

"Okay, sure, no problem. Harlan?"

"Fifty-five million dollars."

"Come on."

"Okay. Seventy million."

Eliza sighed. "Please be realistic, here."

Harlan didn't see the point in trying to be realistic. They had failed to think this plan through. Even if they paid him off, there was still nothing stopping him from going directly to the police. They'd read his blog, so they should have already realized how much he didn't give a shit about being a dickhead. It was in his genes.

But hey, if they wanted to pay him off before they all went to prison, then okay, sure, he'd let them. He wouldn't turn down money, although he seriously doubted its existence in this apartment. But maybe they had some tricks up their sleeves. Maybe one of them had a rich grandmother.

"Okay," Harlan said. "Three thousand."

"Shit," the guy named Stephen said behind them. Louise laughed and whispered something about Halloween decorations again.

Eliza held in her breath before answering. "Okay, three thousand. That's fair. Don't you think so, Nick?"

Nick didn't say anything, just walked out of the living room, into the kitchen. Glass shattered. How precious. A temper tantrum.

"No," Harlan said. "It's not fair at all. In fact, the price should be much higher. But I'm being realistic here. I doubt you can even pay me three thousand, plus enough to fill up Lewis's gas tank? Good luck with that."

"We'll do it," Eliza said. Then, after a moment of hesitation: "And if not, I guess you're right, we could always just kill you."

Then Nick came back into the living room with more duct tape, and seconds later Harlan and Lewis were back in the closet, drowning in their own disgusting odors.

Sexy Cats

"WE DON'T HAVE three thousand dollars," Louise said. They were back in the kitchen, consumed by dread. They were used to dread. It came with the territory of running a small press.

Nick sipped cold coffee and grimaced. "No shit."

"So what are we gonna do?" Stephen asked.

"There are ways to earn money, if we work hard enough."

"Are you talking about whoring?" Louise asked.

"Pretty much." Nick walked into the living room and returned to the kitchen with a stack of paperbacks. "Remember when we needed gas money to get to that Pixies reunion concert?"

Louise laughed. "You want to sell books on the street?"

"It worked last time."

"Last time we didn't need three thousand dollars."

"Well, this time we have more people to help. And a stronger variety of books."

"You're crazy."

"That has nothing to do with anything." He cleared his throat. "Unless anybody has any better ideas, I say this is our best shot. And we need to start moving fast, because let us not forget we have hostages that will eventually be missed by their families."

"Can we borrow money from anybody?"

Nick shrugged. "Doubtful." He looked to Eliza. "Unless you think your mom might help us out."

"Last time we were at my parents' house, Billy stole her jewelry and pawned it all. We aren't really welcomed back at the moment."

"We could always just rob a bank," Louise said, bobbing up and down on her heels, damn near giddy.

Stephen frowned. "You're enjoying all this way too much."

"It's just exciting, is all. How often does shit like this happen?"

"Earlier today you started a riot at the Pic n' Pac."

"And now we have hostages!"

"Jesus Christ."

Nick's eyes lit up. "Wait, that's a great idea."

"What?"

Nick reached into his pocket, then cursed. "Shit. Billy has my phone still. Where the hell did he go, anyway?"

"Probably fleeing the state," Stephen said.

"Or to buy more crank," Eliza said.

Nick reached out to Eliza. "Let me borrow your cell." She handed it to him and he dialed his number. It rang a few times, then he was addressed by his own voice telling him to leave a message. He hung up and called another number.

Sergio picked up on the second ring. "Hiya."

"Serg, this is Nick."

"What are you doing with Eliza's phone?"

"Never mind that. Listen, we're in some trouble here."

"What's wrong?"

"I'll explain later. But I need your help."

"Okay, sure. Whatever you need, man."

"You said you already had a sequel to *The Cumming of Christ* written, right?"

"Yeah, I emailed it to you this morning. You didn't get it?"

"Let's just say I haven't had time to get online today."

"Oh, man. So you didn't see that sexy cat photo I tagged you in?"

"How can a cat be sexy?"

"That tells me you haven't seen the photo."

Nick groaned. "Can you come over to the apartment? Eliza's going to put it up for pre-order right now, but she'll need your help with some market copy, since none of us have read it yet. Plus we'll need a cover."

"Sure, I can be over in a couple of hours. Gonna take a nap first, if that's cool."

"There's no time. We need you over here now."

"What, are you behind on rent?"

"Not exactly."

"I'm pretty exhausted from the reading last night, Nick."

"Please."

"You fuckers better have some coffee made."

"I'll brew a new pot."

Nick gave Eliza back her phone. "Sergio's on his way. While the rest of us are gone, you two are in charge of selling the shit out of *Christ's* sequel. I want our Paypal to fucking explode. Also, put up *The Owls in the City* for preorder."

Eliza raised her brow. "But that's your novel. I thought you were still hoping someone else would publish it."

He shrugged. "I guess I'll just have to withdraw it. Shit, it's gonna get rejected anyway, so what's the point."

Eliza nodded. "We'll do some major pimpage online."

Nick gestured to Stephen and Louise. "We'll head out and start slinging paperbacks. Each of you need to get a crate and fill them with as many books as they'll hold."

Nick reached on top of the fridge and pulled down a jar full of coins, then spread the change among the three. "In case people don't have the exact amount, here you go."

"I don't want to panhandle like a fucking bum," Stephen said.

Louise snorted. "What's the difference between this and when you're begging for a blowjob at two in the morning?"

"I hate you."

"You *love* me."

"I'm gonna need to use your laptop, though," Eliza said. "All of my equipment is at my place."

"I don't care, that's fine," Nick said. "Just remember, you need to sell like you've never sold before. You're gonna need a cover that people won't be able to resist. Whether we face jail-time depends solely on your marketing skills."

"Gee, thanks."

Before they left, Nick said, "Oh, and if your brother shows back up, please do me a favor and break his nose."

"Already planned on it."

"Attagirl."

24.
The Librarian's Daughter's Father

BILLY DROVE THE stolen car to the bartender's trailer, licking his lips, hungry for more drugs. He pounded on the front door for a good five minutes before the bartender finally answered. His eyes were wide with paranoia.

"Who the fuck are you?"

Billy held up his hands, innocent. "It's me, man. From last night? We hung out here and . . . you know, uh, got high."

The bartender shook his head. "I ain't never seen you before in my life."

Billy was getting tired of standing on this porch. "Dude, we met at Nightscapes last night. My friend was giving that reading? Then afterward we came back here and did crank and played PlayStation."

The bartender was quiet for a moment, studying Billy. Then he smiled. "Oh yeah. How's it going, man?"

"Shit's kind of gotten crazy, to be honest."

"Wait a minute," the bartender said, and waited a full minute before continuing. "Where the fuck is my coffee? I thought you were getting me one, too."

"Something . . . came up."

HOW TO SUCCESSFULLY KIDNAP STRANGERS

Billy walked into the trailer and he told the bartender about what happened, told him he had two hostages back at his publisher's house, and he had no idea what to do with them.

"Feed them to human-hungry pigs," the bartender said. "It's how the mafia does it."

"You don't know that."

"I've seen movies."

"This ain't a movie, man," Billy said, although when he thought about it, hell, who knew, maybe it was a movie. Actors never knew they were in a movie. They thought that shit was real.

"So you just left them there?" the bartender asked. "Who's watching them?"

"My sister."

"You don't think she'll snitch on you?"

"Nah, man. My sister loves me."

"All I'm saying is, I used to have a sister, then one day she told my parents I'd gotten some bitch librarian pregnant, and my parents kicked me out of the house. Fuck all siblings."

"My sister's cool."

"Until she rats you out."

Billy sighed. "Whatever, man. You wanna smoke this crystal, or what?"

"Yeah, all right."

Billy and the bartender—whose name was Sebastian—smoked more crank and played video games. Then that got boring, so they started painting the inside of his house blue. The bartender had meaning to do this for some time now, but kept putting it off. Billy tried to forget about the hostages back at Nick's place, but they were all he could think about. If they died, Billy would be a murderer, and he'd go to prison for the rest of his life. He didn't want to go to prison. He was a writer, goddammit. Writers didn't go to prison. They wrote about other people who went to prison.

Writers also didn't kidnap people, especially reviewers who didn't like their work.

Billy was not like normal writers.

He didn't know what he was going to do with his hostages, now that he had them, but he figured if he smoked enough crank then eventually a solution would arrive. If not, then at least he would be too high to give a shit.

Seb asked about the car out front.

Billy nodded. "Yeah, that's the one I stole."

"Ain't you worried about being spotted?"

"I guess I haven't thought about it too much."

"Have you gone through it yet?"

"What do you mean?"

"I mean, maybe there's some valuables in the car. Shit you can pawn, get you out of the country."

Billy frowned, holding the paintbrush, unsure. "Why would I leave the country?"

"Because you're a kidnapper."

"Oh, yeah."

"So?"

"What?"

"Don't you think we should search the car? You never know what you'll find."

Billy thought about it and decided the bartender had a point. He could have kidnapped a millionaire or a celebrity for all he knew. Although, given the type of car the guy'd been driving, he kind of doubted it, but hell, the bartender was right, he wouldn't know for sure until he checked.

"All right," he said. "Let's do this."

Seb grinned. "And, of course, if we *do* find something valuable, I reckon I should get a certain percentage, don't you think?"

"How do you figure?"

"Well, you wouldn't have thought to check if it weren't for me suggesting it to you."

"Fair point."

HOW TO SUCCESSFULLY KIDNAP STRANGERS

They each took another hit and walked outside to the stolen car. Billy popped the trunk and told Seb to check it out while he looked through the glove compartment.

"There's a big ass duffel bag in here," Seb shouted from behind the car. "I wonder if it's full of money."

"Gym clothes seem like a safer bet," Billy said, opening the glove compartment. A handgun spilled out to the floor. He looked at it for a moment, then picked it up and shoved it into his jacket pocket. He didn't say a word.

"Holy shit," Seb cried out. "Holy motherfucking goddamn shit."

Billy stood up and saw Seb backing away from the car. "What the hell, man?"

"I changed my mind," Seb said. "I don't want anything to do with this crazy shit. Fuck this. No way, no fucking way." He turned around and ran into his house. The sound of the lock turning echoed throughout the trailer park.

Feeling the weight of the handgun in his pocket, Billy slowly approached the open trunk. The duffel bag was unzipped and pulled open. Inside, numerous severed human heads stared up at him.

"Oh," Billy said.

25

Paulyshorepunk

I T WASN'T THE easiest thing in the world, to get recognized by passersby while standing on the corner of the street, shouting for attention. Most people assumed you were begging for money, and they would've most likely been correct. It was even more difficult to get attention when you were holding books. People assumed only assholes read books. Maybe they were right.

Nevertheless, Nick stood on the corner of Mellick and Keene, a milk crate of paperbacks at his feet, shouting for people to stop and listen to what he had to say. In his hands he held a sign that said "BOOKS $5", which was cheap as fuck and barely enough to make any sort of profit off the printer's cost, but nobody was going to pay more than five dollars for a book being sold under these circumstances. Hell, even five dollars was asking too much for most people.

The first person to stop was an elderly woman who thought he wanted food. She offered him her leftover sandwich from a nearby café. He accepted the sandwich and asked if she'd like to buy a book.

"A . . . what?"

"A book. You know, like with words? I publish them. And I write some of them, too."

"Books?"

"Books."

"What kind of books?"

"Well, I own a publishing company, and these are some of the books we've released over the years. They're all a bit weird, a bit eccentric. But they're smart. They're entertaining."

The lady glanced at the milk carton, then back at Nick. "What's your company called?"

"BILF Publishing."

She seemed confused. "BILF?"

"Yeah. Uh. It stands for, uh . . . Books I'd Like to Fuck."

She smiled and walked away without another word. Nick called her a bitch under his breath, then ate his new sandwich.

Another older lady showed more interest in the books, until she saw the cover of *Grits & Clits*, then she dropped the book on the sidewalk, told Nick he was going to hell, and ran away.

He managed to stop a man in a business suit shortly after that. The man seemed to be in a hurry, but his eyes lit up at the mention of cheap paperbacks.

"Do you have any James Patterson?" the man asked, after listening to Nick's speech.

"Go fuck yourself," Nick said, and pushed him away.

"Excuse me?" The man stumbled back and caught on to a lamppost to prevent falling. "You have no right to assault me."

"You gave me every right as soon as you mentioned James Patterson."

"What's wrong with James Patterson?"

"Goddammit!" Nick kicked the guy in the ass and watched as he fled down the sidewalk.

Nick sighed, tried to shake off the bad vibes. A group of teenagers approached him, and he prepared himself to kick their asses if they tried to start anything. But they ended up being really interested in the books, and they each bought two paperbacks. Suddenly Nick was forty dollars richer.

After they left, he pulled out his little notebook he always kept in his back pocket and wrote down the title to a potential article idea: "Bizarro—Do it for the Kids".

Someone tapped him on the shoulder. He knew who it was just from the smell alone.

"Jared," Nick said, and turned around.

A filthy, abominable man stood in front of him, grinning a mostly toothless smile. He wore a suit, but it was a suit that had not been washed in years. Maybe the suit fit him once upon a time ago, but now, the buttons were barely hanging on. It would take one wrong move for them to pop off like a cork from a wine bottle.

"What's up, Nick?" Jared said.

"What do you want?" He didn't have time for Jared's bullshit today. Or any day, for that matter.

Jared ignored Nick's question and browsed the milk crate of books on the ground. "Sellin' some books on the street, huh?"

"Always the keen observer, you."

Jared picked up a random novel and flipped through, the way people did when they wanted to feign interest, since there was no possible way anyone would gain any sort of insight on a book through this particular method of browsing, unless you were a pretentious asshole.

"Look," Nick said, "do you even have money to buy a book?"

"Nah. I'm not interested in buying anything."

"Then go away."

"Well, wait a second." Jared dropped the paperback in the milk crate and stood up, groaning as he relieved the pressure from his knees. "I've been meaning to talk to you about some stuff. I tried last night, but you seemed kind of busy. And I was gonna email you, but the library won't let me use their Internet anymore until I take a shower."

"Well, why don't you take a shower?"

"Because of Obama."

HOW TO SUCCESSFULLY KIDNAP STRANGERS

Nick waited for more, but there was no elaboration. "What *about* Obama . . . ?"

"Just . . . you know." Jared shrugged. "Thanks a lot, Obama."

"Thanks for *what*?"

"You know, man. You know."

"Ugh." Nick wiped sweat from his forehead, watching multiple people pass them on the sidewalk. Any one of them could have been a customer, and he blew his chance thanks to this asshole. "Get to the point, Jared."

"Well, as you know, I'm an award-winning editor."

"You have never won an award for editing in your life."

Jared seemed offended. "Back in elementary school, I was given many gold stickers for my outstanding grammar skills."

"What does that have to do with anything?"

"It means I know my stuff. And you should hire me."

"We already have enough editors. I've told you this already. Many times."

"Yeah, but . . . you don't have *me*."

"I don't *need* you."

Nick tried turning away from Jared and focusing on other people, but Jared circled him, not giving up just yet. "Trust me, bro, I have some editing chops. I've edited books for a ton of small presses, all at affordable rates."

"Please go away."

"My last job was editing an anthology that included a story by Lovecraft."

Nick stared at him, unimpressed. "Okay, and?"

"What do you mean? Lovecraft, dude! Not just anyone is hired to edit The Master. Only the best of the best."

"Considering most of his stories are public domain and any asshole can reprint them in the dumbest of anthologies, no, that isn't impressive at all. Sorry."

"You're such a jerk, Nick."

"And yet, you keep trying to get me to hire you."

Jared sighed. "Why do you hate me so much? I've never done shit to you."

"I don't have time for this right now."

"Fine. Eff you then."

Jared kicked the milk carton off the sidewalk and paperbacks flew into the street. Nick thought about leaping at him and tearing his face off, but figured it wasn't worth it. Instead he watched him walk away, whistling. One day he'd get even with that asshole.

Nick stood on the sidewalk and observed as cars ran over the books he'd published. Pages ripped and blew away with the wind.

He gathered the few books that weren't damaged and headed toward Louise and Stephen. Maybe they'd done better. He doubted it.

He made it half a block before he was interrupted by someone else. Not a customer or anyone important, but another goddamn writer. These creatures were everywhere, like cockroaches inside a discarded box of pizza. Like maggots fornicating inside a dried-up corpse.

"Hey, you're Nick Twig, right?" the kid asked. He couldn't have been any older than seventeen. His arms were littered with track marks. His eyes were bloodshot and his breath was strong enough to insult a skunk.

"Yeah, I'm Nick."

"You own BILF Publishing?"

"We aren't open for submissions right now," Nick said, trying to maneuver around him.

The kid held up his hands, stopping him. "Wait, wait, wait. I'm not trying to send you anything. I don't *have* anything."

"Are you going to buy a book?" Nick asked.

"I'm kinda low on money at the moment."

"Then fuck off."

"Wait!" the kid said. "Why are you in such a hurry? I thought maybe we could hang out."

Nick sighed. "This isn't the best day, man."

The kid looked around the city, shrugging at the world. "Yo, there ain't shit happenin' today, just look around. Today's a day to kick back."

Nick laughed. "You and I have had vastly different experiences today."

"Fuck off with what's already happened, yo," the kid said. "Let's talk about right now."

"Okay, what about right now?"

The kid led Nick over to a porch and conned him into sitting down on the stairs with him. "Listen, I'm havin' some major writer problems, and I'm hopin' maybe you can help."

"I don't know why you'd think that."

The kid slapped his knee and grimaced. "Are you or are you not the motherfucker who wrote *The Trampoline Incident*?"

Nick wanted to act irritated and impatient, but at the mention of his book, he suddenly found himself wanting to be best friends with this kid. Someone who dug his work, who he bumped into on the street? Holy crap.

"All right," he said, "what can I help you with?"

The kid cleared his throat. "Okay, well, I'm trying to write a short story for this circuspunk anthology, right? And I'm afraid there aren't enough clowns in it. Plus, most of it doesn't even take place at a circus or carnival. Just, like, one scene. Man, I suck at this. I don't know what to do."

"First off," Nick said, "what the hell is *circuspunk?*"

The kid rolled his eyes. "Circuspunk is a genre for bizarro horror stories that involve circuses and clowns, stuff like that."

"So, horror stories that happen to take place at a circus?"

"Yeah, that's what I said, King of Redundancy."

"That's not a genre. That's just a setting."

"Nah, man, it's totally a genre. You bizarro people made it up."

"Just because someone says something is a genre, that doesn't mean it's a genre."

"And just because someone says something isn't a genre, that doesn't mean it isn't."

"Look," Nick said, "in the beginning of Stephen King's *The Dead Zone,* there is a pivotal scene taking place at a carnival. Does that make the book circuspunk?"

"Well, no, that's just horror."

Nick nodded. "Right, even if the entire book took place at the carnival, it still wouldn't be circuspunk. It's just horror, okay? Horror is an actual emotion, and circuspunk is . . . I don't even know, that's how much this conversation has hurt my brain so far. But even then, who cares? I could argue that *The Dead Zone* was also a political thriller—but why? Do you think when King started writing the book, he was stressing over genre boundaries? Or do you think he was more concerned about writing the best book he had in him?"

"I guess he was more focused on story and character than meeting clown quotas."

"What I'm saying is, these genre rules don't matter. They're pointless. Circuspunk is just horror fiction. Bizarro is just weird fiction. These things already exist, right? I'm going to tell you a bunch of other genres, and you let me know if any of them actually mean a thing: heartcore, paranormal, wetware, retro futurism, SpyFi, slipstream, xenofiction, planetary romance, splatterpunk, slapstick, splatstick, cyberpunk, biopunk, nanopunk, steampunk, dieselpunk, decopunk, atompunk, stonepunk, clockpunk, nowpunk, elfpunk, mythpunk, dreampunk, awakepunk, paulyshorepunk, funkpunk, drunkpunk, spunkpunk—"

"Okay, okay! I get it! Jesus Christ."

"Yes, even christpunk."

"Now you're just making these up."

"Possibly."

"Jerk."

"Definitely." Nick leaned back against the steps, closing his eyes. The sun burned against his eyelids. "But don't you get what I'm saying? You heard all those genres. They all have their own distinctions. Try limiting your story to one of them and it's going to kill you. Blend them all together if you want to. Shove them into a blender and make a delicious smoothie. Don't take it too seriously, do not let it slow you down. Genre will just get in your way. People create these arbitrary rules for writers and none of them mean a thing."

"Nothing means anything. Time is a flat circle," the kid said, staring at him blankly.

Nick groaned. "Ugh, those fuckin' *True Detective* quotes."

"We are all genres created by society."

"Okay, stop being weird." Nick stood up, hands on his hips. "I am going to tell you something right here and now that I want you to hold close to your little heart."

"What's that?"

"Fuck genre."

The kid laughed. "Is that something like fuckpunk?"

"Goddammit, shut up. I'm trying to say something here."

"All right, all right. Shutting up."

"Genre exists to limit writers, okay? You gotta break these walls down. Don't let stereotypes and fictional guidelines silence your originality. Too many writers kill their inner desires to write whatever they want in fear of upsetting potential readers because you didn't follow the exact guidelines of your usual genre. These fears want you to die. Chuck them into a fire and be done with them. There are no rules here. Your main characters do not have to end up together happily ever after in your romance story. The scientist does not have to be mad in your science fiction series. Your male protagonist does not have to ruin your female protagonist's face with cum in your latest erotica. Everybody does not have to die in your horror novel. In fact, nobody has to die. There are no rules in fiction. There is only you and the story. Write from your heart and keep the words true, and forget about everything else."

The kid seemed impressed. "Wow. That was actually pretty good."

MAX BOOTH III

Nick stood up and performed a little bow. "Thank you, thank you very much."

"But here's something I still don't understand," the kid said.

"What?"

"There's a part in my story where one of the characters eats a packet of circus peanuts. Do you think that would be enough to fit the guidelines?"

Nick grit his teeth and said, "Yeah, that sounds fine."

26.
Rise & Fall of the Burger Queen

BILLY STOOD ON the trailer porch for a good ten minutes, pounding on the door and shouting for the bartender to open up. The sound of his pounding was fierce and desperate, but inside, the trailer was quiet and empty. Except of course it wasn't empty. The bartender had locked himself in and he refused to have anything else to do with the situation. Billy didn't really blame him. After seeing the contents of the duffel bag, Billy didn't want anything to do with the situation, either.

But whether he wanted to be involved or not, he was, and now he had to deal with it. A part of him wanted to take off running, leaving the car with its duffel bag of decapitated heads behind. But eventually the police would discover the car, and they'd come knocking on the bartender's trailer. Only this time, Seb would have no choice but to answer. The bartender would surely give up Billy in a heartbeat. It wasn't like they were friends or anything. They'd just smoked together a couple of times and painted a house. He'd done that with dozens of people.

So he got back in the stolen car and drove away. He didn't know where he was going. Certainly not back to Nick's place. The thought of facing the lunatic he'd kidnapped terrified him. Sure, his sister was still there with the guy, and maybe he should have gone back to rescue her before it was too late, but fuck, he was so tired, he couldn't. At least that's what he told himself. And it was partially true. He hadn't slept in over a day, or a week, or a year, he couldn't remember, thanks to the crank horse he'd been riding. He wasn't in any state for a rescue mission.

He gave some serious thought to at least calling Eliza and warning her that she was dealing with some kind of whackjob serial killer, but he just knew she would bitch him out as soon as she answered the phone, and he really wasn't in the mood to be bitched out, especially by his sister, the goddess of all bitching. Besides, Stephen and Louise were with her now. He'd watched them take the hostages inside from the roof. They had the situation under control.

What Billy needed was more crank. With the bartender out of the picture now, he opted to score from his usual source: a Burger King cashier named Samantha who also happened to be a writer, because everybody was a fucking writer.

He met up with her in the Burger King parking lot during her lunch break. She was usually holding, considering the restaurant was her primary selling point. People who ate at Burger King tended to love drugs. Maybe there was a connection. The good thing about Samantha was, since she was a writer, she always gave Billy generous discounts on the off chance that he might convince Nick to publish her. She also wrote positive five-star reviews on Amazon for BILF titles. Billy always assured her he'd talk to him, but he never did.

Samantha slid into the passenger seat of the stolen car, smiling. "Nice ride, man."

"Thanks," Billy said.

"Where'd ya get it?"

"From some serial killer guy."

"Wicked."

"Oh yeah." He paused, waiting for her to cough up the goods, but she just sat there, staring at him. "So, are you holding or what?"

"This car smells."

"Does it?" He sniffed and detected a rancid odor that he previously hadn't noticed. "So it does."

"What the hell is that?"

"Probably the stuff in the trunk. Or maybe I pissed myself. Who knows?"

"What's in the trunk?"

Billy laughed nervously. "Just . . . stuff. Hey, listen, are we gonna do this or what? I gotta get back to Nick's place soon and discuss our publishing schedule."

Her eyes lit up. "Has he read *Burger Queen*?"

Billy looked away, trying to act coy. "Maybe . . . "

"Well shit, why didn't you say so?" She opened her purse and whipped out a pipe. "You can just smoke with me, no charge. Cool?"

"Whatever. Let's just get it going."

They smoked for a few and joked about random shit. He asked her if she had to get back to work, and she found his question to be the funniest goddamn thing.

"Work is for assholes!" she shouted, pounding her fists against the dashboard. She kept commenting on the smell and asking if they could go smoke someplace else.

"Like where?"

"I don't know, maybe my house." She fluttered her eyelashes at him, giving him huge "fuck-me" signals, and it was all Billy needed. They drove away from Burger King and she directed him to her house. Except she didn't really seem to know where she was going. She kept guiding him around in a circle in the same suburban neighborhood, focusing on each house number. Then she'd forget what she was doing until Billy slapped her on the shoulder and asked where she lived.

"Uh, we're getting there."

"Are we lost?"

"No we ain't fuckin' lost," she said, and got all excited and pointed to a two-story house on the corner of the street. "There! Right there. That's where I live. Lost my ass."

"Your ass is lost?"

"It's gonna be lost in your face in a few minutes."

"Shit, girl." Billy tried to pull into the driveway, but instead parked in the middle of the front yard, bashing into a garden gnome. "Whoops."

"Who gives a shit?" Samantha said. "Come on!"

Billy chased after her toward the front door. She tried to open it, but it was locked.

"Shit!" she said.

"What's wrong? Don't you have a key?"

"I left it at Burger King!"

"Shit." He looked around the neighborhood, worried they were making a scene. Just what he needed right now was a bunch of noisy neighbors prying into his business and calling the cops. Fuck that. He needed to stay as far away from the law as possible today.

Samantha grabbed a rock and smashed it through the front door window, then reached inside and unlocked it.

"What the hell are you doing?"

"Relax, man," Samantha said, leading him inside and shutting the door. Glass cracked underneath their feet. "I break windows here all the time. My house, I'll do whatever I want."

"You're crazy."

"That's one perspective." She took off her Burger King T-shirt and threw it at him. "Catch me if you can!"

She turned around and ran through the foyer, down a hallway. He expected the house to be a total disaster, but it was surprisingly clean. Maybe she had a maid. But on a Burger King salary? Wait, she couldn't even afford this house on a Burger King salary. Maybe her dad was rich. Although she *was* a drug dealer, so . . . who knew? Who *cared*?

HOW TO SUCCESSFULLY KIDNAP STRANGERS

Billy followed her into the kitchen. She'd stripped the rest of her clothes and was bent over the fridge, scavenging through its contents. Her flat, pancake ass taunted him. It said, "Come smack me, Billy. Come squeeze me."

"Okay," Billy replied.

"What?" Samantha said.

"I said, do you have any beer?"

"Uh, I dunno, doesn't look like it. I guess I'm a prude. Oh wait, here we go."

She stood up and spun around, holding a tall bottle of wine between her breasts.

"Isn't that cold?" Billy asked.

"That's the best part!" The bottle was half empty. She took a long swig and passed it to Billy. He didn't really care about wine, but it was better than nothing, so he gulped it down despite the overly sweet kick in the face, and his belly warmed and his erection stirred.

Samantha continued running around the house and Billy followed. She eventually led him upstairs to the master bedroom. He noticed multiple photographs of a black family hung up on various walls, but his attention was more focused on Samantha's bouncing tits. He tackled her on the bed and she giggled as he kissed her neck. The foreplay only lasted a couple seconds before he grew impatient and stuffed himself inside her. He started thrusting like a rabid dog and for a moment he forgot all about kidnappings and heads in duffel bags. But only for a moment. They were soon interrupted by the sound of a woman screaming downstairs.

Billy stopped thrusting, but remained inside her for a moment. "Who the hell is that?"

Samantha stayed quiet.

"This isn't your house, is it?"

"How should I know?" she asked.

"You're fucking crazy, girl."

"Come on, finish!"

"No! We gotta go."

"Fuck you, you pussy."

Billy pulled out and put his pants back on. "We gotta get out of here before the police show up."

Samantha sighed. "Fine, but I'm taking a souvenir."

"What?"

Samantha hopped across the bedroom and, rolling on tiptoes, reached up and pulled down a large wedding photograph of a man and woman.

"Who are these people?" Billy asked.

"I don't know," Samantha said. "But they belong to me now."

"That's some evil-sounding shit."

"I'm an evil girl."

Naked and holding on to the wedding picture, she sprinted out of the bedroom and down the stairs. Billy followed, watching her nonexistent ass as he ran. A woman stood in the doorway, talking to someone on her cell phone. Billy recognized her from the wedding photograph. She'd aged at least a dozen years and had put on some considerable weight, but she was definitely the same woman.

She screamed and shouted into the phone, "Yes, I see them now! They're trying to escape! Please hurry! One's a man and the other's a wom—"

Samantha swung the wedding photo and the glass shattered against the woman's face. She fell to the floor, unconscious.

"Holy shit," Billy said, and ran for the car.

"Pop the goddamn trunk!" Samantha said. "I don't want to be holding this photo all day."

Billy got behind the wheel and pressed the trunk release button, and it was only when Samantha started screaming that he remembered what was still in the trunk.

"Uh-oh," he whispered, and cautiously stepped out of the car. Samantha was still standing there, but now she'd dropped the wedding photo. Her eyes were glued on the contents in the trunk, on the opened duffel bag, and the numerous severed heads inside.

HOW TO SUCCESSFULLY KIDNAP STRANGERS

Billy held up his hand, trying to calm her. "Now, before you freak out, I can explain."

Samantha realized he was standing next to her and screamed louder. "Help! Somebody help! Oh God, help me! He's a psycho! He's gonna kill me!"

"Will you please be quiet? It isn't as bad as it seems."

Samantha turned around and tried running away, but Billy grabbed her and pulled her back. "Just wait a fucking second so I can explain what's going on, will you? Jesus fucking Christ."

"HELP! HEELLLLPP! SOMEBODY HEEEEEELLLP MEEEEEE!"

Billy sighed. "Okay, but this is your fault."

He pushed her into the trunk and closed it, locking her with the collection of human heads. Police sirens were closing in. He punched the steering wheel until his knuckles bled and then he drove away.

27.
Asscracks of the Universe

LOUISE WAS TOO excited to be standing on the sidewalk trying to sell people books. She wanted more action. She needed more thrills. More gas station riots, more random kidnappings. Fuck this vanilla pedestrian bullshit.

Stephen, meanwhile, seemed to be content on the sidewalk, panhandling to strangers. She guessed he preferred this to being back at the apartment with a couple of guys tied up in the closet.

She wasn't stupid. She knew they weren't meant to be together forever. They'd never exactly had much in common, besides both being available and being connected to the small press scene. Stephen was easy, sometimes a little clingy, but predictable enough to keep as a boyfriend for a short while. After so long, though, predictability ran dry—usually around the time that you become involved in a hostage situation.

When the foot traffic was light, Stephen would pull out his camera and snap photos of random objects. Louise asked what the hell he was doing and he said with the right angle, anything in this city could be a book cover.

"Sure," Louise said. "That split in the sidewalk could be for my next book, *Asscracks of the Universe*."

"Or it could represent the cracks in a relationship, being stepped on countless times a day by strangers."

HOW TO SUCCESSFULLY KIDNAP STRANGERS

"Yes, of course."

Louise stopped a man walking past them and said, "Hey, dude, if you buy a book I'll flash you my tits."

"Louise!" Stephen said.

"What if I buy two?" the guy asked.

"I'll let you take a photo."

"Deal."

The guy grabbed two random paperbacks from their milk crate, handed them ten dollars, and took a photo on his smart phone of her exposed breasts. Stephen stared at the scene, shocked, but then he took a photo, too, so fuck him and his false outrage.

Louise decided just to keep doing this until she either ran out of books or she was eventually arrested. A few cops passed her, but they only slowed down long enough to get a good look, then they drove away. The milk crate emptied. They'd made ninety-five dollars.

"Who would have thought that whoring yourself out was profitable?"

"Many people," Stephen said. "That's why there are so many sex workers in the world."

"God bless the whores."

"Sex workers."

"Shut up."

"Now what?" he asked.

"I guess we'll go back to the car and refill on books."

"Are we gonna be doing this all day?"

"Are you kidding? We're never gonna stop."

Stephen pouted and walked away. Louise followed. They made it half a block and bumped into a homeless freelance editor eating leftover McDonald's from a trash can.

Louise tried to turn around and walk in the opposite direction, but Stephen didn't get the hint.

"Jared!" he shouted, and ran up to him.

Jared pulled his head out of the trash can and smiled at Stephen once he targeted the source of interruption.

They pounded their fists together like true hardcore gangsters.

Louise sighed and joined them. "Hey."

"So, you guys are out sellin' books too, huh?" Jared asked.

Stephen nodded. "Yup."

"I ran into your boy, Nick, earlier." He pointed behind him. "He was a real asshole."

"He can be that way," Stephen said.

"Nick is a saint," Louise said.

Jared ignored her and spoke directly to Stephen. "So, I was trying to talk to him about you guys possibly hiring me for my editorial skills."

"Yeah, Nick really does all of the editing. I don't think he's looking to hire anybody."

"Maybe you could talk to him?"

Stephen hesitated, took a step back. "Well, he doesn't exactly listen to me. And I already know, on this subject, he definitely isn't interested."

"What does he have against me?"

"Uh. I dunno, man."

Louise coughed. "Liar."

"What was that?" Jared asked.

"Oh. Nothing."

Stephen gave her a dirty look. She smiled.

"Maybe if he would just let me do a test edit, he'd see how good I am."

Stephen scratched his head. "Yeah, but, like, didn't he hire you to edit some novella a few years ago?"

"Yeah, and I did amazing work. So I don't understand his problem."

Louise couldn't hold her breath any longer. She gasped for air. "Dude, you can't edit for shit."

"Excuse me?" he said.

"Louise!" Stephen said.

"I'm sorry, but it's true. You don't have any idea what the fuck you're doing, and everybody knows it. Nick, along with anyone else worth their salt, dislikes you because you claim to be this all-wise editor, yet you barely have a grasp of the English language. Did you never learn grammar in school? For fuck's sake, dude, even basic spelling you have trouble with. And that would be bad enough by itself, but you constantly scam new writers and publishers into paying you for your services, and they have to learn the hard way that not everybody in this business knows what the fuck they're doing. They would be better off flushing their cash down the toilet."

Jared stared at her, speechless. Stephen looked at his feet, cheeks blushing. "Uh, maybe we should go."

"Yeah," Jared said, tears streaming down his face. "I think that would be a good idea."

Louise burst out laughing. "Jesus Christ, dude, are you crying?"

"Leave me alone."

Stephen grabbed her arm and pulled her along. "You're such a dick," he said, and in response she laughed even harder.

Nick was waiting for them at his car. The trunk was open, and his milk crate of books were still full.

"You didn't sell shit, did you?" Louise said.

He shook his head. "I see you made out well."

She nodded. "Yeah. I started flashing my tits."

"Ah. Good idea."

"I can't fucking believe you," Stephen said to Louise. "He didn't deserve any of that."

"Oh fuck you, he did too and you know it. Goddamn hustling trash artist."

Nick seemed confused. "Who didn't deserve what?"

"Jared," Stephen said. "Louise made him cry."

He laughed. "You made him cry?"

Louise grinned, proud. "Hell yeah. It was beautiful."

"I can't believe I missed that."

"You may get to relive the moment," Stephen said.

Nick raised his eyebrow. "How do you figure?"

"He is charging straight for us."

"What?"

Stephen pointed down the block. Jared, in all his glory, was running like a mad bull directly toward them.

"Holy shit," Louise said, giggling.

Nick shook his head, amazed. "Well, this ought to be good."

"You assholes!" Jared screamed from down the street. "You motherfuckers!"

"I do believe he intends to murder us all," Nick said.

"I didn't even do anything," Stephen said.

Louise snorted. "Story of your life."

"We are officially broken up," Stephen said.

"Whatever. Jared's gonna kill us, anyway."

"He seriously might," Nick said. "He is a rather big man."

"And incredibly slow."

"Yeah. That, too."

They stood in the parking lot and waited patiently. They felt it was the polite thing to do, after insulting him so much.

"I'm getting tired," Nick said. "I wish he'd hurry up."

"If he kicks your ass, will you hire him to edit?" Louise asked.

Nick thought about it, then nodded. "Yeah, probably so."

"So that's the secret."

"That's the secret."

Jared neared. He continued shouting threats. His running had declined to a brisk walk, and he kept holding his chest like he was two seconds away from a heart attack.

"Gon . . . na . . . fuck . . . ing . . . rip . . . your . . . heads . . . off."

Jared, finally in the parking lot, pushed himself into another sprint toward them. For a moment, Nick thought they might be in some serious trouble, but then Jared tripped over his own untied shoelaces and tumbled to the cement. His pants fell down and his bare, hairy ass flopped out for the world to see. His skull smacked against a concrete parking stop and his body went limp.

They stood above his body for a moment, staring at his ass. It was mesmerizing, like a shooting star fueled by flatulence.

"Well," Nick said. "That was anticlimactic."

"Do you think he's dead?" Stephen asked.

"Probably."

"I think he's still breathing," Louise said.

Blood began pooling under his head.

"We should probably call an ambulance," Nick said.

Stephen shook his head. "Why? The hospital isn't that far. Let's just drive him."

"I don't want that piece of shit in my car."

"Dude," Stephen said, "he's bleeding out the skull. Cut him some slack."

Nick sighed. "Ugh. You fucking owe me, man."

Stephen smiled. "I knew you had a soul."

They were barely out of the parking lot when Louise's cell rang. It was Eliza.

"What up, girl?" Louise said.

"Uh, you guys need to get back to the apartment. Now."

"Okay, sure, give us a few. We gotta drop Jared off at the hospital."

"Fuck that," Eliza said. "Get your asses back to the apartment."

"What's going on?"

"Sergio's dead."

28.

The Cocks in the Closet

ELIZA HATED USING Nick's laptop. Pubic hairs were always lodged into the keyboard. She'd told him before that he sucked at cleaning up post-masturbation, and he'd just giggle and tell her to write him a post-apocalyptic book about sex addicts.

Sergio had already emailed them the sequel to *The Cumming of Christ*. She took one look at the title and started laughing, which was definitely a good sign. She browsed through the manuscript, reading a few lines here and there, getting a sense of the general plot. It sounded just as ridiculous as the original book.

The cover idea for *Cunnilingus is Close to Godliness* came almost instantly. She started up Photoshop and got to work. She tried not to think about the fact that there were two men tied up in the closet, but it was difficult, especially when they began pounding on the door and screaming through the duct tape. She ignored them for a little while and continued working.

The screaming progressed. It grew louder and more desperate. Could the neighbors hear? Shit, that was all she needed. Cops knocking on the door because of a noise complaint. What a pathetic way to get caught.

She opened the closet. Only one of the hostages was screaming—Harlan. The other hostage, Lewis, was grabbing Harlan's cock with all his might. He'd turn around so he could latch on with his hands still tied behind his back.

"What the hell are you doing?" Eliza said, and tried to pull Lewis off him. But he was quicker than she expected. He released his grip on Harlan's cock and smashed his face into hers. She stepped back a few feet and tripped over some books on the floor. Fucking Nick, she told him he ought to clean this place up once in a while.

Eliza tried to stand up, but Lewis jumped on top of her, leaving her lightheaded and gasping for air. He did this with his hands still tied behind his back. Who *was* this guy? Before she could defend herself, he was standing above her and kicking her ribs. Then he stomped on her face and she passed out.

She woke up with her arms and legs tied behind her back, like a goddamn hog. Harlan was next to her, bloody. Her face throbbed. It felt wet and deformed. Maybe he'd broken her nose, kicked it straight into her brain.

Lewis was sitting on the floor a few feet away, out of breath. In one hand he held a knife and in the other he held a beer.

"That man had been lying," he said. "He did too have beer."

"What are you even still doing here?" Eliza asked. "Why haven't you run away?"

Lewis sipped the beer, looked at her, contemplating the question, then took another sip. "My car is missing. I don't intend to leave until I retrieve it."

"Have you called the police?"

He shook his head. "It's not them I have business with."

"My brother."

"If your brother is the man who kidnapped me and stole my car, then yes."

"I think you broke my nose."

"And soon I will remove your head from your shoulders."

They stared, daring the other to speak. Neither did, except for Harlan, who screamed through his duct tape. As if reminded of something, Lewis tossed the empty beer bottle to the floor and stood up. He found the roll of duct tape by the sofa and crouched down next to Eliza, then wrapped it around her mouth.

"I know it isn't much," he said, "but at least it'll slightly dampen the sound of your screams. And believe me, you will be screaming quite a bit here soon. You and that buffoon I've spent all day locked up with."

Eliza tried to curse at him but it all came out as nonsense through the duct tape.

"They always scream," he said. "And I don't blame them. Decapitation is a hell of a way to go out, especially when it's all slow and drawn out."

Eliza's eyes widened with terror. She wanted to kick Nick in the balls for leaving her here alone. Then she wanted to strangle her brother for kidnapping a goddamn psychopath. A part of her was still hopeful, though. She wasn't dead yet. Maybe the guy was just bluffing. He didn't *sound* like he was bluffing, but who really knew. Plus, in the movies, whenever the bad guy gave a long speech about how he was going to kill the protagonist, he almost never had a chance to follow through with it. That's why horror slashers like Michael Myers always got his shit taken care of. No talking. No dumb speeches. Any second now, help would arrive. Or he'd slip up and offer an opportunity for her to bash his brains in with something.

"First, though," he said, standing up, "I would like another beer."

Lewis walked into the kitchen just as the front door opened and Sergio entered the apartment, obviously ready to save the day. *See? That's* why you didn't give big speeches before you murdered somebody. Fucking amateur.

HOW TO SUCCESSFULLY KIDNAP STRANGERS

Sergio stood in the doorway, staring at her, and she tried screaming for him to turn around and run away, to call the cops before her hostage—wait, who was the hostage now?—decapitated everybody. But he just stood there like an idiot until Lewis returned to the living room and drove a knife through his throat.

She was reminded of the way a hose might spurt water from the side of the tubing if a hole was poked into it. Only instead of a tube, she was staring at a neck, and instead of water . . .

29.
Bizarro Sorrows

AFTER HIS READING, Sergio decided to stay up and ride the energy high. He sat in his apartment with his laptop and wrote. Various horror movies played in the background. He'd pay attention to a scene here and there, but he was mainly absorbed in his writing. He was pretty drunk, but alcohol had never really made him tired. It woke him up. Gave him the creative spark that helped pay his rent.

He walked home from Nightscapes and immediately started writing a new novel. Or maybe it would be a novella. He didn't know and didn't care. All he knew was he had a killer idea for a story and he would write it until the story ended, then he'd send it to his publisher, and maybe he'd make a couple hundred bucks in royalties in six months or so. Or maybe he'd make nothing.

The book, obviously inspired from last night's events, was about a zombie outbreak during a public book reading. It was fast paced and bloody as hell. And, like most of his books, it took place in the span of one day. The best stories—especially suspenseful stories—took place in short bouts of time. Books that went on for years and years were boring as hell. If the story was supposed to continue past a couple of days, then he'd just write a sequel.

By that afternoon, Sergio had already written fifteen

thousand words. Most writers wouldn't have even started their outlines by then. But most writers were cowards. A lot of people Sergio knew weren't even real writers. They just liked to pretend. They talked plenty of talk on Facebook and offered recycled writing advice on their blogs, but they never wrote anything worth reading. Some of them didn't write at all. They just talked about it.

That was the difference between Sergio and most of the people in the small press scene—Sergio actually did his job. What other small press author was consistently putting out solid material? Hell, the year was barely halfway over and he already had nearly twelve books released. Twelve books *this* year. Total? Shit, last time he counted, he was almost to sixty.

Meanwhile, everybody else was on Facebook, talking about writer's block and boasting over pathetic word count goals. Fuck word count and *especially* fuck writer's block. Writer's block did not exist. It was just an excuse to be lazy.

If you wanted to be a writer, you couldn't afford to be lazy. You had to be like Sergio and treat it like any other job. It was when you started acting like it was different from normal jobs that things started going south. If you treated writing like a typical nine to five, then you would get the work done. But if you acted like you were a special snowflake who was better than everybody else, then you weren't gonna get shit accomplished. If you worked at Walmart, you couldn't sit around and wait for inspiration to kick in. You either stocked the shelves or your ass was canned. Sergio held the same philosophy about writing. He knew he wasn't special. Nobody was special.

When he was first starting out and still spoiled like everybody else, he had a certain mantra he'd repeat every day before writing. After so long, his words finally stuck, and now he was finally being productive

You am not special.

You do not deserve leniency.

You are an employee of the mind. You wanted to work, well here's your chance to work. Now work.

You are no different than the kid who flips burgers at McDonald's.

You are the garbage man outside your house.

You are the person scraping road kill off the side of the highway.

You do not get a speed-pass to skip ahead in line. There is nothing remarkable about you that differentiates you from any other soul out there trying to make a dollar.

You are a person with a job to do. You either do your job, or you're fired. You sit around, fucking off, complaining enough, then they'll just find someone else to do it.

You don't feel like writing? Too bad. Do you think the waitress down the block feels like busting her ass, listening to your problems, only for a two-dollar tip? No, but she does it anyway. Why? Because she has a job to do. She wants to get paid. Your worries are pathetic in her eyes. She doesn't sit around and wait for something to inspire her to refill your coffee.

Every second you aren't writing is another second you're wasting on the clock. What are you even doing here?

You may not have a spatula or a box cutter, but you do have a pen, you do have a keyboard. Your tools may be different, but it doesn't change the fact that your shift isn't even close to over.

So either shit or get off the pot.

So that's what Sergio was doing.

Well, he *was* doing his job. Now he wanted to sleep. But something had come up. Nick needed him over at his apartment right away. They were putting the sequel to *The Cumming of Christ* up for pre-order already, which was strange, since the first book only came out a few months ago. His publisher hadn't sounded like his normal self. Something was wrong. Maybe he owed somebody money, and he was being threatened. Sergio considered the possibility, then wondered if maybe he could turn that idea into a novella. He would call it *Bizarro Sorrows*.

HOW TO SUCCESSFULLY KIDNAP STRANGERS

Sergio got dressed, gathered his laptop and USB stick in his messenger bag, and walked across town to his publisher's apartment. He didn't have a car. Cars were for people who had places to be. The only place Sergio needed to be was at home, writing. Or at his uncle's cabin, also writing. Except when his publisher randomly demanded his presence. But such times were rare. And besides, Sergio didn't mind walking. Walking was good for you. It was the best way to brainstorm future books.

If *The Cumming of Christ* continued to be such a success, then the sequel, *Cunnilingus is Close to Godliness,* would be a hit. His fans would demand a third one. He certainly had ideas. Hell, the way his buzz was going lately, he could continue this series for the rest of his life. Writing sleazy stories about Jesus just came naturally to him.

It was weird, how word-of-mouth moved for *The Cumming of Christ*. When it was first released, it got shared around on Facebook and Twitter like it usually did. A few laughs here and there. It moved up the ranks on Amazon. The same as his other books. Nothing too special, but still decent for a small press weird fiction author. But then, almost two months after its release, there was an article hitting all the usual news websites. A high school English teacher in Washington had been fired for assigning *The Cumming of Christ* as required reading for his students. The news story went viral, and soon *The Cumming of Christ* was in the top one hundred of most sold books on Amazon. Well, for a few hours at least, and then a James Patterson book knocked it back out. But still, Sergio's book was selling. The article was being shared even today. More copies were being moved. He had no idea who this teacher was, but he pretty much saved Sergio's life. He couldn't wait until that first royalty statement. It already tasted sweet and delicious.

Sergio eventually made it across town, still thinking about turning *The Cumming of Christ* into a trilogy. Nick's car wasn't in the parking lot, but the apartment was unlocked.

Inside, Eliza was on the floor, hogtied. Next to her was another man, also hogtied. Their faces cried blood.

Sergio stood in the doorway, frozen. A guy walked out of the kitchen, into the living room, smiling. He held a knife.

"I haven't seen you yet," the man said.

Sergio had no words.

"Where are the rest?"

"What . . . "

"Ah, well." He lunged at Sergio before he could figure out what was going on, driving the knife into his throat and making his world wet and hot.

30.
Twack

SERGIO COLLAPSED TO the floor and Lewis kept stabbing him. It dawned on Eliza that he was trying to saw off his head, but he was having a hell of a time, considering his tool of choice was a shitty steak knife.

She almost vomited, but managed to keep her ill down. Vomiting with your mouth sealed was a sure way to choke to death. And she wasn't about to die today. Instead she started bobbing herself back and forth until she built up enough momentum to roll herself over, then she continued rolling until she made it into the kitchen, out of sight of the vicious bastard in the living room. The duct tape had loosened a bit. She kept moving around until it loosened enough and she was finally able to break free.

She scrambled to her feet and scanned the kitchen in a hurry. Lewis would notice her absence any second now, if he hadn't already. She picked up a frying pan from the sink and ran back into the living room. The sick sonofabitch was still on top of Sergio, cutting at him. She spotted the dildo crucifix on the floor next to them and her eyes widened. She lowered the frying pan and picked up the crucifix, preferring its weight. She raised the new weapon and smashed it against the back of his head, expecting him to go unconscious like they did on TV. Instead he cursed and stood up, giving Eliza a mean stare.

"That stung," he said, and stabbed the knife at her. He missed completely, leaving himself open for another twack from the dildo crucifix. This time a tooth flew out of his mouth. He stood in place, temporarily dazed. Eliza took advantage and started smashing the dildo crucifix into his face over and over until he stopped moving.

She picked up his knife and threw it across the living room, disgusted. She grabbed the duct tape and taped his hands behind his back, using up the rest of the roll. How the fuck did he even get himself untied last time? She looked around, saw his belt on the floor. It'd been ripped in half, like he'd been picking at it all afternoon until the fabric finally gave.

The front door was still wide open. If anybody walked by, they'd discover a scene that'd make Eli Roth come in his pants. Eliza grabbed Sergio's feet and dragged him inside, crying and wishing none of this was real. She closed the door and locked it. She found a blanket and threw it over Sergio's face. The sight was awful. Everything was so goddamn awful.

She needed out of this apartment. Surely somebody had heard them and called the police. There was no way in hell all of that had gone unnoticed.

Eliza called Louise on her cell, told her to get their asses back here and pick her up. Shit had hit the fan and they had to figure out a new game plan pronto.

Five minutes later, the front door knocked. She unlocked it, expecting to find Nick and the rest of the group.

"Hey, sis," Billy said.

1
Paperback Graveyard

JOSEPH COULD NOt believe a high school teacher had actually assigned *The Cumming of Christ* as required reading to a class of teenagers. He was all about expanding what children and teenagers were allowed to read in school, but holy shit, *The Cumming of Christ* was a fucked-up book. He had never read anything quite like it before. It was intriguing. It was filthy. It was perverted. It was gross. It was beautiful.

The fact that this book was published seemed completely ridiculous and, at the same time, kind of inspiring. It showed that no matter how weird you really were, there would always be freaks just like you to back up your ideas.

Joseph looked the author up on his smart phone while sitting at his speed trap. Sergio Placid had over sixty books in print, and he was supposedly only twenty-seven years ago. How was that even possible? Joseph was almost forty and he hadn't accomplished shit.

What Joseph really found interesting, though, was that Placid actually lived in the same town as he did. In fact, the majority of the publishing company that produced Placid's books lived here, too. He wondered if he ever arrested any of them before. They could be anyone, really. Joseph had no idea. He wanted to believe the company consisted of upstanding citizens, but seriously, anyone who approved of something like *The Cumming of Christ* was one depraved animal.

He wondered what that said about himself.

A new call came on his radio. A noise disturbance at a nearby apartment. Of course he was called to the scene. Everybody else was busy. Joseph wanted to say he was busy, too. This book was really grabbing him.

He set it down and drove to the apartment, knowing if he hadn't answered the call he would be in even deeper shit than he already was with his captain. A door on the ground level of the apartment was wide open. He stood in the entrance and shouted his presence. Nobody answered. He peered inside and lost his breath at the sight of a man sprawled out on the carpet floor. There was a blanket over his face, but the blanket was drenched in what looked like blood. The carpet below him was also soaked in the same red liquid.

"Oh shit," Joseph said, and radioed for backup. Then he stepped into the apartment, gun drawn. He was going to have to shoot somebody. He couldn't do it. It wasn't in his genes. He wasn't a killer. Fuck. Why did he take the call? He should have just stayed at his speed trap and continued reading *The Cumming of Christ* in peace.

But it was just him and the corpse. He discovered dozens of paperbacks scattered on the floor. Some had blood soaked into their pages. He recognized many of the covers. They belonged to titles the Books I'd Like to Fuck company had published. They all did.

That was a little too much of a coincidence for Joseph to handle, so he walked outside and puked into some bushes and thought about the meaning of life. He could be home right now with his dachshund and everything would be okay. Instead he had chosen to get dressed and go to work, and this was his punishment. Maybe it was God playing an evil trick. Or maybe it was just destiny, going on as scheduled.

HOW TO SUCCESSFULLY KIDNAP STRANGERS

Later, once Joseph discovered the identity of the corpse in the apartment, he decided he would officially put his two weeks' in.

32.

A Warm Welcome

"**Y**OU MOTHERFUCKER."

Billy tried to look innocent, but the bullshit was in such abundance it was practically seeping from his eyeballs. "What?"

Eliza didn't answer. She punched him in the face. Hard. His face exploded with blood as he covered himself with his hands, crying.

"Shit, sis, I think you broke my nose."

"Well, now you and I match."

He removed his hands and looked at her and seemed to realize for the first time how gory she was. "Holy shit, who did that to you?"

Eliza thought about punching her brother again, but her hand was still stinging from the last one, so instead she stepped aside and gestured to the tied-up hostages on the ground. Specifically, Lewis.

"You went ahead and kidnapped a deranged psycho."

Billy nodded. "Yeah, I already figured that out. Sorry about that."

Eliza eyed him strangely. "How?"

He laughed. "There's a bunch of severed heads in the trunk."

"How is that funny?"

"It's not."

"Then why are you laughing?"

"Because otherwise I will kill myself."

Eliza stared at Lewis on the ground, still unconscious. Or, at least, he looked like he was unconscious. Maybe he was playing possum. She looked back to her brother, only now realizing the gravity of his words.

"Did you say there are *heads* in the trunk?"

"Yeah."

"*Whose* heads?"

"I don't know." He shrugged. "Just a bunch of heads."

"Are you high?"

"Yeah."

She was still having a difficult time comprehending the situation. "Heads. In the trunk."

"Yes."

"How many?"

"Quite a few."

"Who the fuck drives around with heads in their trunk?"

Billy nodded to Lewis. "That dude, apparently." Then he noticed Sergio on the ground. "What happened to Sergio?"

She pointed at Lewis. "He fucking killed him."

"Shit."

"Yeah, dude. Shit indeed."

"What are we gonna do?" Billy asked.

"I thought maybe you'd know, considering you're the one who got us all into this situation."

"Maybe we should call the police."

"I don't really want to go to prison, Billy."

"True."

"Nick's on the way. We can figure out what to do when they get here. Unless the police are coming because of all the noise we just made before you showed up, in which case we are screwed."

Billy sighed. "Maybe we should just leave, tell Nick to meet us someplace else."

"Like where?"

"I don't know. Doesn't Sergio's uncle still have that cabin in the woods? That might be good."

Eliza smiled, her face dripping blood. "That's actually not a bad idea."

"Should we take Harlan?" he asked, gesturing to the squirming hostage on the floor.

"Yeah, might as well. But we'll leave the psychopath here for the cops to collect."

"Wait," he said. "Is he awake right now?"

"I don't know."

"What if he heard us?"

"So fucking what if he heard us?" Eliza asked.

"Well, he could tell the cops we're going to Sergio's uncle's cabin."

"Like the cops know where that's at."

"I'm sure they could find out."

"I don't want to drive with that guy in the car with me."

"We can put him in the trunk." Billy paused, then pulled out the gun he'd taken from the glove compartment. "Or I could kill him, I guess."

Eliza gasped and backed away. "Where the fuck did you get that?"

"His car."

"Of course you did."

"So, what do you think?"

She threw her hands up in the air, defeated. "All right, fine. Throw him in the trunk. I don't give a shit."

"And we'll keep Harlan in the backseat?"

"As long as you keep the duct tape over his mouth."

"Deal."

Billy bent down and started dragging Lewis out of the apartment. Before he left, he told Eliza to steal some clothes from Louise's room.

"I already planned on changing," Eliza said. "I'm all covered in blood and shit."

"They're not for you."

HOW TO SUCCESSFULLY KIDNAP STRANGERS

"Uh, okay." She stared at him, afraid to ask who they were for. Unfortunately, he answered the question anyway.

"The clothes are for Samantha."

"Who the fuck is Samantha?"

"The girl in my trunk."

"One of the . . . heads?"

"Well, she has a complete body. A naked one."

"She's alive?"

"Yeah."

"How the fuck did she get in the trunk?"

"Well, don't get mad, but—"

"—*Billy*—"

"I had to kidnap her, okay?"

She punched him again.

What Will Our Mothers Think

LOUISE HUNG UP her cell and told Nick there had been a change of plans, they were all meeting up at Sergio's uncle's cabin.

"I thought Serg was dead."

"I'm just saying what they told me, okay?"

"That cabin's like a half hour away, at least."

Louise sighed. "Well, you better drive faster then."

"How the hell can Serg be dead? What the fuck is going on?" Nick said, more to himself than anyone else. The world was melting around them and there was nothing they could do about it.

Stephen tapped his shoulder from the backseat. "Um, what are we going to do with Jared?"

Nick cursed. "At this point, we're way past the hospital. We'll just kick him out of the car at the next stop sign."

"You can't do that!" Stephen said. "What if he dies? We can't leave him out on the street by himself."

"Oh, fuck him."

"Nick . . ."

"Fuck, all right. We'll take him to the cabin and he can die there and then you can bury him in the woods. Happy?"

"I don't think I'm ever gonna be happy again."

"I can't believe Sergio's dead," Louise said, quiet.

"So the one guy, the one that isn't Harlan, just

snapped?" Nick asked. "What did you say about heads in a trunk?"

"The car, the one Billy stole. He found heads in the trunk. The guy's a serial killer or something."

"Jesus motherfucking Christ."

"Don't mention Jesus," Louise said. "It makes me think of Sergio."

"I think we're way over our heads, guys," Stephen said.

"Shut the fuck up, Stephen," Nick said. "That kind of talk doesn't do anything to help us."

"I'm just saying."

"Yeah?" Nick looked behind him, taking his eyes off the road. "And what do you suppose we do with that bit of wisdom? No fucking shit we're in over our heads. That doesn't mean we can just press a RESET button and start the day over. We're in this shit whether we want to be or not, and now we're gonna deal with it the best we can."

"And how are we gonna deal with it?" Louise asked.

"I don't know."

"I don't want to go to prison," Stephen said. "My mom's gonna be so angry."

"Nobody's going to prison," Nick said.

Louise whimpered. "Sergio . . . "

Nick sighed, squeezing his fists around the steering wheel until his knuckles whitened. "Fuckin' Billy."

4.
Improv

THEY TRIED BRINGING Samantha to the backseat and getting her dressed so she didn't have to ride in the trunk with the psycho, but she wouldn't listen to reason and kept screaming no matter what they tried to do to calm her, so eventually they had to surrender and stuff her back in the trunk with Lewis and his heads.

Harlan sat in the backseat. His hands remained duct taped, but they removed the tape from his mouth. They figured it'd be kind of suspicious looking if any passing cars happened to glance inside.

It took a while to calm Harlan down. He kept staring at Sergio's body and screaming. Eliza didn't blame him. She kept crying, too. Shit was fucked-up.

"We have to go to the police," Harlan said. "This is really serious."

Billy turned around from the passenger seat and told him to shut his mouth. "If we started listening to your opinions, then we'd never write again and all go jump off bridges. Isn't that what you said in your blog?"

Harlan threw his head back against the seat, groaning. "Will you imbeciles forget about my blog for one moment? A man has *died*. He was *murdered*. You need to go to the police."

"We never said we weren't," Eliza said, focusing on the road ahead, afraid that if she looked elsewhere she'd burst out crying again. "But first, we're going to the cabin so we can meet up with everybody else, then we'll figure out what to do. We just need some time to think."

"What's to think about? Go to the police. What's wrong with you people?"

"We're gravy-brained retards," Billy said. "According to you, at least."

Harlan groaned again and kicked the passenger seat. "You immature asshole. I hope you rot in prison for this."

Eliza drove. The rest of the ride, everybody was mostly quiet. When a pounding started rising from the trunk, Billy turned up the radio to drown out the noise. Eliza didn't like leaving Lewis and Samantha in the trunk together, but she didn't know what else to do. This wasn't her typical routine. This was improv at its finest. Besides, who the fuck was Samantha, anyway?

The cabin was unlocked because there wasn't a lock in the first place. Billy dragged Lewis into one of the bedrooms, wrapped his body with more duct tape (they'd made a stop at Dollar Tree on the way over) and threw him in a closet, then propped a wooden chair under the knob. Harlan, not in any mood to escape, just walked into the cabin. A cloud of dust exploded as he planted himself on the couch in the living area. When Billy walked back outside to retrieve Samantha, he found the trunk empty. He looked down the driveway and saw her naked ass running halfway down it.

"Shit," he said, then she flipped over another car turning into the long, dirt driveway.

5.
That Was No Deer

NICK SLAMMED ON the brakes. "What the fuck was that?"

"A deer?" Louise suggested, peering through the now cracked windshield.

"You both know what that was," Stephen said.

Nick ran his hands through his hair, shaking. "Shit. Shit, shit, shit."

He got out of the car, looked at the blood all over the hood, cursed some more. He walked down the ditch branching from the driveway, into the weeds and bushes. A naked girl lay in the thick of it all, covered in blood. Her eyes were open but she wasn't seeing.

Someone was shouting down the driveway. He looked up, saw Billy running toward them, waving his hands in the air. Nick climbed up the ditch and proceeded at a calm pace toward Billy. The closer they came to each other, the more fucked-up Billy looked. His face was broken and bloody. Nick didn't care. When he was close enough, he kept his mouth shut and ignored the words coming out of Billy's mouth. He stared at Eliza's druggie brother, not thinking, just trying to hold back a mountain of rage and failing to prevent the avalanche. He speared Billy onto the dirt driveway and started pounding into his face, cursing at him and telling him how he'd screwed everybody over, they were going to prison because of his stupid ass, and he was going to murder him right here in this driveway.

If it wasn't for Stephen and Louise breaking them apart, he really might have done it.

Louise noticed the dead girl in the bushes. "Who the fuck is that?"

"Ask him!" Nick shouted, pointing at Billy.

Coughing blood, Billy sat up. "That's Samantha. She's a girl I know."

"What was she doing out here?" Louise asked.

Billy scratched his head. Dirt clouds floated out of his hair. "Well, you know, one thing led to another, and to keep her from going to the cops, I had to throw her in my trunk. Well, Lewis's trunk."

"You kidnapped her?" Nick said, pushing Stephen off of him and lunging at Billy again. He got one good punch in before Louise and Stephen managed to pull him away. "Stop fucking kidnapping people, you asshole!"

The back door of Nick's car opened, and Jared stepped out, groggy, holding his bleeding head wound.

Billy eyed him, confused. "What's he doing here?"

Nick went quiet.

Louise laughed. "Shit," she said. "I guess we kidnapped him."

36.

Everything Ends at
A Cabin in the Woods

"WHERE'S THE NAKED CHICK?" Eliza asked as they returned to the cabin.

"Dead," Billy said.

She stood on the porch, staring at them, silent.

Billy gestured behind him, at Nick. "Our faithful editor-in-chief hit her with his car."

"Fuck."

"That's about the gist of it."

"So now we're murderers on top of kidnappers."

"Next on the list: terrorists," Billy said, walking past her into the cabin.

Nick stayed outside, dazed, looking at the setting sun.

"Are you all right?" Eliza asked.

He shook his head and held his hand out to Billy. "Give me my phone."

"A 'please' would be nice."

"I am going to fucking murder you."

Billy handed him his cell. Nick stuffed it in his pocket and walked off into the woods, not saying another word.

"Where's he going?" Stephen asked.

"Climb a tree, wrestle a bear, take a shit, who knows,"

Louise said. "Just let him be. Dude just killed somebody. That has to bruise your soul."

"What's Jared doing here?" Eliza asked.

Billy began laughing. "He was kidnapped!"

Eliza nodded. "That makes sense."

"You two look like shit," Louise said.

"Eliza punched me," Billy explained. He held up two fingers. "*Twice.*"

"And what happened to her?" Louise nodded to Eliza's bloodied face.

Eliza pointed to a closed bedroom. "That fucking lunatic attacked me, right before he half-decapitated Sergio."

Everybody fell silent in the cabin, the image of Sergio looming above them all like a black cloud casting a great rain upon the earth.

Jared was walking around in short circles, staring at his opened palm and becoming mesmerized. Blood dripped from the gash in his skull like snot from a toddler's nose. Eliza asked him if he wanted to sit down. He responded by drooling and asking for some toast, then he fell down on the couch and started snoring heavily. His head rested in Harlan's lap.

"Did you say the woman you kidnapped has been killed?" the book reviewer asked.

"That's none of your fucking business," Billy said.

"This situation is going to continue to spiral out of control until you call the authorities."

"Fuck the police."

Harlan shook his head. "I believe it is you who is going to get fucked."

"Not before I gouge your stupid eyeballs out of their sockets."

"Afterward, are you going to bury my body with your other victims?"

Billy collected the duct tape and wrapped it around Harlan's mouth, then he sat down in a recliner, satisfied with his work.

"I want to see these heads I've been hearing so much about," Louise said.

"Now's not the time," Eliza said. "We need to figure out what we're going to do."

"Should we wait for Nick?"

"Fuck him," Stephen said. "If he doesn't want to be here, then we can make a decision without him. He isn't our father."

"What are we going to do now that Sergio's dead?" Eliza asked.

"Same as what we're doing with everything else," Billy said. "Moving onward."

"Yeah, until you want to get high again," Stephen said.

"True." Billy paused. "I didn't mean for any of this to happen."

Harlan laughed from behind the duct tape, and in unison, they told him to shut the fuck up.

"Maybe we should just give up," Eliza said. "Turn ourselves into the police."

"No offense," Louise said, "but that sounds like a pretty dumb idea."

"Maybe they won't be so hard on us if we surrender willingly. They might even be relieved we helped them catch that head-collecting psycho."

"We've still kidnapped a shit ton of people. Plus we have a dead girl out front now."

"Well, then what do we do?" Eliza asked. "Try to sneak out of the country, live the rest of our days in Mexico? We're all broke as shit. I assume the book selling didn't go over too well."

Louise shrugged. "I sold a decent amount."

Stephen laughed. "Yeah, after showing a sea of men your tits."

"It worked, didn't it?"

"Do I even want to know how y'all ended up with Jared?" Eliza asked.

"He was being his usual jerk self," Louise explained. "You know how he can be."

Eliza nodded.

"I don't want to keep driving around with hostages and severed heads," Billy said. "It's freaking me out."

"Well, why did you start?"

"It seemed like a good idea at the time."

"I'll give you this," Louise said. "It's definitely been an interesting day."

"I mean, I have this gun." He pulled out Lewis's handgun to show everybody. "Maybe we should just shoot Harlan and Lewis, and I guess Jared too, and then start driving very far away from here. Live life on the road. Do what sis said and go to Mexico. Mexico wouldn't be too bad. I love churros."

"Where the fuck did you get a gun?" Stephen said, backing away.

Louise's eyes lit up. "Holy shit. Badass."

"It's Lewis's."

"He's probably murdered a ton of people with that," Stephen said.

"I figured as much."

"Then what are you doing with it?"

"I don't know." Billy examined the gun like it was an alien object fallen from the sky. "I guess we'd be better off with it than him, considering we're the kidnappers and all."

Billy made a solid point.

"I don't want anyone else to die," Stephen said.

"Even the motherfucker who killed Serg?" Billy asked.

Stephen looked away, unable to respond. Nobody could respond. They couldn't say what they all thought because what they all thought was madness and confirmed their inner psychopaths.

The group broke apart to explore the cabin. Canned food was stored in the pantry, along with a few cases of bottled water. The cabin didn't have electricity, so they started lighting candles and lanterns as the sun fell and the moon rose.

There wasn't much to do in the cabin. Sergio's uncle

never came up here anymore. Sergio would visit once a month to go on a writing retreat. It was his favorite place to work. Out in the wilderness, away from society. No internet, no TV, no distractions. This cabin was his paradise. And now he was dead, and it was all Billy's fault.

Eliza would never forgive him. And she was his sister. The rest of the group must have hated his goddamn guts. She didn't know how long she'd be able to protect him— she didn't know if she *wanted* to protect him. He had brought this misery not only upon himself, but the rest of the company, as well. He had killed their futures singlehandedly. Their lives as writers and publishers were forever shattered, like a bullet through a mirror.

Louise and Stephen went into an empty bedroom and shut the door. Eliza didn't know if they were fucking or sleeping or what. Billy pushed Jared on the floor and lay down on the couch, resting his head on Harlan, who'd already started to doze off. Billy wasn't about to sleep anytime soon, she could see that plain as day. He lay there, shaking, blinking like the air was electric. Guy was too pumped up on whatever was in his system. He would never sleep again at this rate.

She wondered where Nick had gone. She doubted he'd left them. He was probably just walking around, collecting his thoughts, trying to come up with a plan that wasn't piss-poor pathetic, unlike the rest of them.

In movies, the criminals always had these master plans that sounded brilliant. Yet, nobody could think of shit to do besides sit around and wait for something to drop in their laps. It was pretty sad. What was the point of wasting their lives watching movies if it wouldn't help them when it really mattered?

All Eliza knew was there was no way she was tired. For one thing, she was starving. Everybody else had to be hungry, too. Nobody had eaten anything all day. All they'd had was bad coffee. She went into the kitchen, took some aspirin she found in a cabinet, then sorted through the canned food in the pantry. She got out some bean drip and Tortilla chips, ate a few, then pushed the food aside. She was hungry, but the process of physically moving her mouth and swallowing seemed too overwhelming right now. Maybe she was tired, after all. Maybe she was more tired than she'd ever been in her life. She left the food on the table in case anybody else wanted some. She briefly considered bringing a plate to Lewis, but decided the psycho didn't deserve food. He could starve in that closet for all she cared.

She went outside and sat down on the porch and stared at the night sky. In the darkness, everything was calm.

37.
Small Press Outlaws

NICK WALKED THROUGH the woods debating never returning to the cabin. This didn't have anything to do with him. He hadn't kidnapped anybody. Well, okay, he'd kidnapped Jared, but nobody gave a shit about Jared. And, all right, he might have killed a random girl with his car, so maybe he did have a lot to do with the situation now, but goddammit, he didn't want to be involved. This wasn't his fault. Why the fuck did they have to bring those assholes to his apartment?

There was no longer a simple solution to this problem. The bribery plan was shot out the window as soon as Sergio was murdered. Driving to the cabin, a million thoughts running through his head, Nick was sure of one thing: once he got a hold of that sick fuck Billy had kidnapped, the one who'd savagely murdered Sergio and undoubtedly others, he would drag him to the police station and turn him in. Then Nick would confess to everything that had happened and pray for them to go easy on him. Nick had a company to run, and he sure as hell couldn't run it if he was an outlaw.

But now? Well, that was all shot to hell as soon as Billy kidnapped yet *another* person and Nick killed her with his car. Now there was no going to police. He would have to deal with this himself.

HOW TO SUCCESSFULLY KIDNAP STRANGERS

He kept checking his email on his cell, but the signal out here was awful. It was doubtful that the publisher he submitted his own novel to would be contacting him at this time of night, anyway. It was doubtful they'd be emailing him tomorrow or any other day, too. Obviously his book was going to be rejected. Maybe they wouldn't even send a rejection. Maybe it was so bad, the book didn't warrant an email letting him know just how bad.

Like it really mattered at this point. They could accept it, sure, but he'd be in prison long before he was given a chance to sign a contract, and he seriously doubted any publisher would want to do business with a convicted murderer and kidnapper. Although, Nick hated to admit it, if the tables were turned, he would go out of his way to sign on a controversial case such as his own current situation. People would eat that shit up and he'd probably sell a ton of copies. But not everybody had the same kind of balls as he did. People were too afraid of being offensive. That's why Nick dug the small press scene. They just didn't give a shit.

Was there a way to get out of this without going to prison? Nick doubted it. They could try to flee the country, but would they make it across the border? And if they did, what then? It wasn't like they were flowing in cash. Where were they going to get money? Maybe they'd fully embrace the outlaw life and start hitting up liquor stores and gas station across the US on their way to Mexico. Go out with a bang.

The idea seemed surreal and ridiculous. Nick wasn't an outlaw. He was barely a writer. And he was even less of a publisher. He was nothing.

Except now, he was a kidnapper. He was a murderer.

Last night, he had his whole life ahead of him.

Less than twenty-four hours later, he was closing in on a dead-end with no room for a turn-around.

Where to go from here? Nick didn't know. He was just going to keep walking until an answer came to him, and if an answer never arrived, then his feet would start getting sore.

He wondered what his mom would say when she found out. Would she understand? Did she understand when he got arrested for fighting in that bar? Or the time he got drunk and stole an inflatable Santa?

He could already hear her lecture. He decided once he was arrested, he would refuse her visitation rights. She didn't need to see him behind bars and he didn't need to see her judging him for shit that wasn't his fault.

Shit like running over and killing a woman. A woman who was still somewhere in those bushes, now a midnight snack for the forest's wildlife. They couldn't just leave her there. She was a human being. Billy said her name had been Samantha. He knew a few Samanthas in town. Only one of them was blonde, like the one he'd seen in the bush. Although he hadn't taken a good look at the dead girl's face, he was willing to bet she was the same Samantha who worked at Burger King. She was known around town as a good source for bad meth. And if she was in the meth business, then it was likely Billy and her were acquaintances.

She hadn't been that old. Early twenties at the most. Her body would continue to age, but her mind would not. Her flesh would deteriorate but her heart would no longer beat.

Why was she naked, anyway? What the fuck was Billy planning on doing with her? He'd never trusted Eliza's brother, but now he was afraid of him, too. Only a fool didn't fear a man riding a crank binge.

If anybody was arrested, it should be Billy. Maybe they all should be arrested, but Nick didn't like the sound of that. Billy was too dangerous to be left alone. He needed to be locked up. Him and Lewis, except Lewis was different. Lewis wasn't even human. Him and Billy differed in that Billy didn't know what he was doing, he was just too high to realize the consequences of his actions. He could be helped for this sickness. Lewis, on the other hand, couldn't be helped. He was a murderer. A serial killer, if the rumor about the severed heads was true. A sick deviant needing to be put down. Nick didn't want to be the one to have to put him down, but he didn't know who else would be up for the job. Hell, he'd already killed one person today. What was another?

But how would he do it? Slice his throat? No, fuck that. That was way too graphic. Just thinking about it made Nick want to be sick. Maybe he could just poison his food or something. There was bound to be some rat poison or some other toxin floating around Sergio's uncle's cabin.

Nick sat down on a log at the thought of Sergio.

Sergio had been a good man. More importantly, he had been an amazing writer, and Nick had been truly lucky to exclusively publish his work. Sometimes Nick felt guilty publishing him, because he knew he could never truly market and promote Sergio as he deserved. Sergio was a writer who needed to be read by thousands, not be dozens. With the recent controversy involving *The Cumming of Christ*, Nick was positive Sergio would finally receive his long-owed recognition. And maybe he would, but now it would be found postmortem. And maybe that was all right, in a fucked-up way. The best writers didn't get recognized until their deaths. Maybe now it was Sergio's turn to be a legend. A mascot for the new breed of degenerate writers. He would be what Sonic was for Sega, but for small press literature.

As he sat on a log, leaning back against a tree stump and looking at the polluted sky, Nick came to a decision. He would kick Billy out of the group. Tell him to turn himself in to the police or fuck off someplace else; he no longer wanted anything to do with his toxic ass. Then he would put Lewis down for the big sleep, feed him some poison or pour bleach down his throat, something, who gave a shit, really; the man was a monster and deserved to be put down as such. He'd let Harlan go, but not before punching him in the face for all the shit he'd said on his blog. He had no idea what he'd do with Jared. Maybe by the time Nick returned to the cabin he would have bled out from his head wound.

Nick would try for Mexico. Or maybe Canada. He'd ask Louise, Eliza, and Stephen if they wanted to join him. If they didn't, then fine, whatever, they'd go their separate ways. If they did, then tomorrow, after taking care of everybody else, they would plan their trip. If they didn't leave by tomorrow, they might as well turn themselves in. Hell, tomorrow might already be too late. He had no idea how much the police already knew. They might not have even found Sergio's body yet.

When he made it back to the cabin, there was another car parked in front of the cabin. Billy was outside, on his knees with his hands raised high. Standing in front of him was another man, one Nick didn't recognize.

In one hand the man held a pistol and in the other he held a severed head.

38.
Aim for the Head

JOSEPH NOUS GOT off work at 6:00 P.M. and he couldn't stop thinking about Sergio Placid. He'd stopped reading *The Cumming of Christ*. Every time he tried to continue he would break down crying. Sure, Sergio wasn't the first corpse he'd seen, but goddammit, this one had struck a nerve. All day he'd spent reading his words, and to randomly stumble across his murdered body? Joseph had never been a very spiritual man in the past, but after today, shit, who wouldn't be?

When he made it home, his dachshund, Lucy, was waiting in the doorway to greet him. She ran around in a frenzied loop, tongue out. Deep down, Joseph knew she was only excited to see him because his presence meant somebody was finally available to open the back door and let her outside to pee and bark at birds.

He escorted her to the yard, then stumbled into his bedroom and took off his uniform, changed into more casual clothes. A frozen Hungry Man would accompany him tonight for dinner. Instead of Netflix, however, he'd resort to the Internet for entertainment. Sergio Placid had a semi-popular blog about writing that he'd update twice a month. It would never be updated again. Joseph wondered if Sergio's fans were aware of his demise yet. Was his family?

MAX BOOTH III

The last blog post Sergio had written had been about the death of the reclusive writer and the rise of the whore. The whore being, of course, the writer who threw himself or herself out in the wild and did whatever it took to get their work read. The kind of writer who wasn't just a writer, but an editor, a publicist, and just about anything else one could imagine.

Joseph read the article as he shoved forkfuls of microwaved mash potatoes into his mouth, the sound of Lucy barking in the backyard as background.

```
"Shoot Your Readers in the Head"
        by Sergio Placid

You're surrounded.
The living dead circle you like
bicycle bullies around the fattest,
foulest child in the school. There's
not many bullets left in your pistol,
so you have to make every shot count.
If you even slip up in the slightest,
these things are going to eat you
alive. They'll rip out your guts and
breathe in your entrails. There is no
time to waste. Take them out before
they turn you into a sandwich and move
on to someone more interesting.
Raise your arm. Tighten your finger
around the trigger. Aim for the head.
Shoot.
There are no do-overs. There are no
time-outs. The time to act is now. So
shoot.
Now imagine all these drooling
flesh eaters are potential readers,
and each bullet in your gun is an
opportunity to be read. An opportunity
```

to be successful, whatever successful even means to you. There is a finite amount of opportunities in the world, so you have to make each shot count.

You have to aim for the head.

Destroy the brain. Convert the reader.

There are certain misconceptions about the world of writing. Readers without any actual connection to the writing industry often assume writers are rich, and that every single book published hits bookstores worldwide and sells like stolen perfume bottles outside a Wendy's (I've had strange encounters behind Wendy's).

There's a reason a stereotype exists that involves parents not wanting their children to become writers. It is not just a silly fear—it is a legitimate concern for their children's wellbeing. Professional writing is no joke—it is extremely difficult to make a living off your words, especially if you publish with a small press. You have to bust your ass, and even then, it probably won't be good enough.

It will never be good enough. But you can try.

But how can one writer market to thousands of potential readers? Simple—by starting off small. By planting your seed into one reader and allowing your fiction to gradually grow and spread through many more. I realize how gross "planting your seed into one reader" sounds, and I do not regret my phrasing in the slightest.

You have to appeal to readers. When you realize that you're not just selling your book, but yourself as a human being, then you can start taking your career seriously. Always remember, the book is not the product—you are the product.

Get out there and interact. Show the readers you're someone worth reading. Show them you are a person.

The day of the reclusive writer is dead. He shot himself over an embarrassing lack of sales.

Joseph let Lucy back inside and refilled her food and water bowls. He returned to the table with a fresh beer, scrolling through Sergio's blog. This was a man who knew what he was talking about. Someone who wasn't fucking around. Joseph had never possessed any interest in writing before, but reading Sergio's articles on the craft made him sincerely believe he could do it, if he disciplined himself well enough.

Joseph found another interesting blog post, not so much about writing advice, but about his favorite places to write around the city. He said unlike most writers, he despised writing in public. Sergio figured the kind of writers who liked writing in Starbucks didn't actually like writing, they just liked being seen as a writer. Sergio preferred doing his writing in seclusion, without interruption. He did a lot of it at his apartment, but he admitted that the Internet ate up a lot of his time. No, his favorite place to write was a cabin his uncle owned. It was out in the woods, away from civilization. No Internet, no electricity, no anything. He would go up to the cabin every month with a stack of notebooks and write like a crazy person, then go back home the next week and type everything he'd scribbled down. Most of the time, he was able to write one or two novellas over the weekend. Some people went fishing for relaxing vacations. Sergio went writing in his uncle's cabin.

Fascinated that there could be such a spot somewhere close by, Joseph logged into the police database and searched Sergio's profile. He found his uncle, then looked up the man's known property. The cabin wasn't difficult to find. It was about a half hour away from Joseph's house.

Joseph leaned back in his chair and thought about the cabin. It was up there in the woods, empty. Sergio would never again step foot in it. He would never write again. The thought made Joseph incredibly depressed. He wondered when Sergio's uncle would return to the cabin. Did he know about his nephew's death yet?

Joseph finished his beer and thought about it some more. He was putting his shoes on before he realized what he was doing. He got in the car and started driving, still not fully aware that he was driving out to this dead man's writing utopia. He didn't know what he was going to do when he got there. He just knew that he wouldn't be able to sleep tonight until he at least saw it in person. And maybe if it was unlocked he would take a walk around, get a feel for it, sit in the same places Sergio had sat, maybe even whip out a notebook and write like Sergio had written.

Joseph had never felt so inspired in his life.

Imaginary Lovers

"I'M GOING TO call the police."

Louise stared at Stephen, fists balling up, resisting the urge to strike him. "You are not calling the police."

Stephen sighed, pacing the bedroom. He had dragged her in and shut the door shortly after arriving at the cabin. Louise thought he was going to fuck her or something. But apparently he just wanted to bitch.

"I swear, I'm the only one making any goddamn sense around here," Stephen said, "because you've all lost your minds."

"How you figure?" Louise asked.

Stephen looked at her like she was an idiot. "People have died, Louise. Sergio was murdered. Nick ran over some girl with his car. Who's gonna die next, huh? Because it's bound to happen again. And again. That's our life now, unless we call the police and put a stop to all this."

All Stephen ever did lately was whine about everything. Louise couldn't stand it. "I don't understand how I was ever attracted to you."

"That's a real nice thing to hear," Stephen said. "I'm trying to be serious here."

"If we call the police, we will be arrested. I do not want to be arrested. Neither do you. It isn't that complicated, dude."

"How can you say that? Kidnapping? Murder? This isn't *simple*."

"Sure it is." Louise nodded. "Murder is the simplest thing on the planet. And the most natural. One moment you're alive, then the next you're not. Just like the way God intended."

"I'm not talking about dying from natural causes here. I'm talking about murder."

"We are all murdered in the end," Louise said, "and God is our murderer."

Stephen threw his arms up in the air, groaning. Then he knocked a pile of books off a dresser. The whole cabin was littered with paperbacks, which seemed to be an ongoing theme in the places he visited. "Now's not the time for your mind trips, Louise. Goddammit, why is everything a game to you?"

She shrugged. "I guess because in the end, what the hell does it matter? We're all gonna end up like Sergio, anyway. So fuck it."

"It doesn't have to be that way," Stephen said. "Last night, after the bar, don't you remember what a great time we had together? We stayed up, making love . . . wasn't it wonderful?"

"I was pretty drunk."

"You're pretending like you were too drunk to remember what happened, but that's bullshit. You never blackout. You remember, and I know you felt something."

"Yeah, your dick."

"More than that. You know what I mean."

Louise was quiet.

"I know we don't get along all the time, Louise. I also know we get along better when it's just me and you and there's nobody else around. It's like you put up this defensive shield, and you don't want anybody to know you have emotions, that you could possibly be in a relationship with anybody else. Well, I know better than that. I know you love me. And I love you, too, despite all the mean things you've said to me lately. I know you didn't mean them, that you were only saying those things because you were afraid. There's no reason to be afraid. It's okay to love me."

Stephen had moved closer to her now, kneeling on one knee and maintaining eye contact. Almost like he was proposing to her or something. Louise couldn't help it. She started laughing.

Stephen frowned.

"What's so funny?"

"I'm sorry. It's just that you're . . . too romantic."

"And that's a bad thing?"

She nodded. "It is when you've created the romance in your head."

"What do you mean?"

"Dude, the girl you were just talking about? That wasn't me, I don't know who that was except some imaginary fuck-dream. You have no idea what type of person I am, you just project this stupid chick flick girlfriend who doesn't even remotely resemble me. You're a hopeless romantic, and no, that isn't a cute quirk. It's an annoying mental disorder. Admit that we don't have shit in common besides the publishing company and let's just move on with our lives. We were good fucks and that's about it."

Stephen's eyes became wet and tears started dripping down his cheeks. He looked pathetic.

"Stephen, come on . . . "

Stephen shook his head, biting his lip. He turned around and ran out of the bedroom.

She sat on the bed, not giving a shit if she ever saw him again. Then she heard him scream.

40.
Dat Ass

BILLY TRIED TO sleep, but it was pointless. Experience told him that he hadn't been awake nearly enough days yet to reach a relaxing enough state of mind to be able to sleep. He couldn't exactly remember how long he'd been awake at this point. After so long, time ceased to exist. Sleep was a fairy tale. His eyes were cracked rocks. The world was his playground, but he didn't have the energy to play.

He stayed on the couch for a while with his eyes closed, resting his head on Harlan's lap. He hated the man with a passion, but had to admit he made a comfortable pillow. He couldn't get his mind off the contents of Lewis's trunk. Whenever he closed his eyes, he saw them. They were calling for him. Like they were these fucked-up sirens guiding his brain into the ultimate crash. He kept thinking the heads belonged to him, that Lewis didn't exist, it was Billy all along who owned the collection. They were his rewards and he was neglecting them in a hot trunk, letting them rot. He was a terrible head owner. He didn't deserve them and they didn't deserve him.

But then Billy turned slightly on Harlan's lap and whacked his face with a surprised erection, and he screamed. He jumped up and pointed accusingly at a confused Harlan. "You perverted bastard! I was trying to rest!"

"What are you talking about?" Somehow the duct tape had peeled halfway from his mouth. "I was sleeping."

Billy made a disgusted grimace and exited the cabin. His sister was sitting on the steps, looking at the sky. He sat next to her and wrapped his arm around her.

"You okay?" he asked.

"I suppose I could be worse. What about you?"

"I keep thinking about those heads," he said, staring at Lewis's car, eyes glued on the trunk.

"What about them?"

"Who do you think they belonged to?"

"His victims, obviously. The sick fuck."

"I know that, sis, but I mean, do you think they were chosen at random? Or were they his friends, family, what?"

"Why don't you go ask him?"

Billy shook his head. "I don't want to be alone in the same room with him. He terrifies me."

"He *should* terrify you. It would be strange if he didn't."

He let her words drift in the air for a moment, then said, "What are the chances of accidentally kidnapping a serial killer?"

Eliza laughed, then frowned. "That motherfucker murdered Serg right in front of me. He enjoyed it. He would have done the same to me if I hadn't gotten myself untied in time."

"I'm glad you did."

"Maybe if I had been quicker, I could have saved Serg, too."

"I think you did the best you could."

"But it wasn't good enough."

Billy knew he should have been a good brother and continued to offer words of comfort, but he was too obsessed about the heads to think about anything else important. Because nothing else *was* important. The universe began and ended with the heads. They weren't always severed heads, hiding in a trunk. Once upon a time, they had belonged to complete bodies. They'd rested atop shoulders. They were special. Now they were nothing. The idea that he too could have been one of those heads consumed Billy. That was no way for anybody to go out. What would happen to those heads now? What was Lewis planning on doing with them? Probably some sick perverted psycho shit. Some weird, Patrick Bateman snuff film shit.

It was weird, how they were just sitting in a duffel bag. Why not put them on ice or something? This was no way to take care of your severed head collection.

He wondered what the police would do with the heads if they got busted. File them in some evidence lab? Store them away in a police station basement? Would the heads be given a proper funeral?

What if they were never found? Were these heads Billy's responsibility now?

What was he supposed to do with a bunch of heads? He'd never been taught how to handle these kinds of situations. He was just a trailer trash writer with a sweet tooth for crank. He wasn't in the disposing-of-severed-heads business. Hell, he wasn't even in the kidnapping business until this morning, and look how badly he'd already fucked that up.

Eliza had stopped talking. He looked to his side. She wasn't sitting by him anymore. Maybe she'd gone back inside after she realized he wasn't paying attention to anything she was saying. Oh well. Fuck her. Fuck everybody. They all hated his guts now, anyway. Like he meant to get them all mixed up in this clusterfuck. If anything, it was Eliza's fault for making him come pick her up for lunch. He had tried telling her he was busy, but no, she needed her stupid cheeseburger. Yet here he was, getting pissed on because he had the nerve to throw a couple people in his trunk. Like he knew one of them was a serial killer. Shit. What Billy did on his own time was his business. Next time he saw Eliza, he would be sure to bring that up. Fucking nosy-ass people.

In the meantime, there were still those heads in the trunk. The heads who hadn't hurt anybody. Well, okay, Billy didn't know that for sure. Those heads could belong to a bunch of child molesters and dog fighters, he didn't know. But he had a hunch they were innocent, at least as innocent as a person could be, which in all truth wasn't really that much, when you thought about it. But screw that. Nobody deserved to have their head pried from their body and thrown in some dirty trunk. Something needed to be done.

Billy got up, opened the trunk of Lewis's car. The heads stared up at him, waiting impatiently for him to take action.

"Avenge us," the heads said in unison. "Kill that bastard."

"Shut up," Billy said.

"Cut his head off and throw it in the trunk with us. Give us five minutes alone with him."

"I said shut up, I'm trying to think here."

"It's fucking hot in here! You left us alone. We can't breathe!"

"You don't have any lungs."

The heads began laughing. "You got us! There's no getting past you."

"You guys are a bunch of assholes, aren't you?" Billy said.

"Hey, Billy, Billy-boy, you got any more crank? Huh, Billy? What do you say?"

Billy thought for a moment. There might have been some in the front seat that Samantha had left behind. No. He couldn't. He shook his head violently. "I can't keep doing this shit. It's killing me."

"You're already dead," the heads said.

"No I'm not."

"You might as well be in this trunk with us. Come on in. We can scoot over, make room for you. Bring the crank, it'll be a party up in here."

HOW TO SUCCESSFULLY KIDNAP STRANGERS

Billy stared at them, refusing to blink. Their mouths opened at the same time, and one voice left their gruesome throats in unison, like they were one creature, one being.

"You guys aren't really talking," Billy said, giggling. "None of this is real."

"Billy, Billy-boy, Billy-billy-billy-boy, don't you see? Don't you see?"

"Stop it."

"Don't you see we're the realest goddamn things this universe has ever offered?"

"I'm not even here. I'm back home, in bed. I'm asleep. My eyes. Oh God, I'm so tired. Oh fuck."

"Crawl in with us, Billy-boy. Crawl in and we can have an orgy. We can fuck like mythological beasts. Bring your sister. You know you always wanted to tap dat ass."

"No. I can't."

"*Tap dat ass. Tap dat ass. Tap dat ass. Tap dat ass.*" They sang the words like a Christmas carol.

"You bastards. I was going to rescue you."

"What's the matter, Billy-boy? Don't you want a little head?"

They stuck their maggot-infested tongues out and licked their lips, making loud, revolting slurping noises.

"Shut the fuck up!" Billy shouted.

"Who you talking to, boy?" a man asked behind him.

Billy spun around, wide-eyed, and found himself face-to-face with a bona fide demon. No, not a demon. Just a man, a man holding a gun. A gun pointed straight at him.

Hell, he could've been a demon. Who said demons couldn't use guns?

"You a demon?" Billy asked.

The man gave him a queer look. "No, I'm a police officer." He brushed his jacket aside, flashing a badge attached to his belt. "I'm gonna have to ask you to put that firearm down."

"What?" Billy said, then realized he was holding

Lewis's gun. How long had it been in his hand? Shit. He threw it to the ground. "Sorry."

"That's all right," the cop said. "Now step aside."

Billy did.

The cop approached the trunk, peered inside, then yanked his head back, gagging.

"Oh my God, oh my God."

He stepped forward again, reached inside and picked up a head by its hair. He stared at it for a moment, looking at Billy, then the head, and tossed the severed body part back into the trunk. He looked like he was about to puke. Billy didn't blame him.

"What the shit," the cop said.

"I know," Billy said. "I don't know what I'm supposed to do with 'em. Any idea?"

The cop emphasized the gun in his hands, told him to get down. Billy obliged.

"What the fuck are you doing with those heads in your trunk?"

"They were in there when I acquired the vehicle."

"Yeah, that so?"

"Yeah."

The cop handcuffed Billy, then dragged him to his own car, which Billy somehow hadn't noticed until now.

"Man, you drive quiet."

"I think you were too busy talking to those heads."

"They started it, man."

"Who else is in the cabin?"

"Nobody," Billy said. "It's just me."

Somebody screamed inside the cabin.

"Nobody, huh?" the cop said.

"I think I need to speak to an attorney."

41.
Hostages & Hostages

PEOPLE THOUGHT DUCT TAPE was unbreakable. Those people were idiots. If you knew what to do, you could get out of duct tape just as easily as scotch tape. And Lewis knew what to do. The real trick wasn't getting out of the duct tape, it was getting his hands from behind his back to in front of him. After he conquered that goal, the rest would be a piece of cake.

Except he wasn't going to be freeing himself inside the closet. There simply wasn't enough room. He started pounding his shoulder against the door. The wood splintered instantly. Five more good whacks and the door was shattered open, the chair propped in front of him tumbling to its side.

He flew into the bedroom, into the darkness. There were no lights on, no candles lit, nothing. He didn't mind. The darkness was his friend.

Fortunately, Lewis had ridiculously long arms. Lying on his back, he bent his knees and arched his ass up, giving enough space to slide his tied-up hands down his body, over his feet, and to the front of his torso.

Sometimes it paid off to be flexible.

Lewis stood up, raised his arms over his head, then brought them down as hard as he could manage, yanking his hands apart in the process. The tape loosened, so he did it again, and again, giving him enough room to slip one hand out of the restraints and peel it off the other hand. This was too easy.

He slowly moved across the room, hands reaching out, feeling for the wall or the door or *anything* that wasn't the infinite emptiness of darkness.

He found the door relatively quickly, pulling it open quietly. Candlelight greeted him from down the hallway. Lewis walked toward it, slowly, relying on tiptoes to avoid obnoxious creaking. He made it halfway down the hall when a bedroom door next to him opened and a man walked through it. Lewis didn't hesitate. He lunged at him, tackling him against the wall. The man screamed. Lewis punched him in the face, then wrapped his hands around his neck and pulled him up, dragging him back into the bedroom he'd just escaped from. His freedom was now evident to everybody in the cabin. Progressing toward them would do no good, especially when one of them now had his gun. Instead, he'd return to the darkness and wait for them to come to him. Now that the hostage had his own hostage, anything was fair game.

These fuckers were going down.

"Let me go, goddammit," the man said.

Lewis tightened his grip around his neck. "I suggest you silence yourself before I do it for you."

He continued backing up until he made contact with the wall opposite the door. He slid down into a sitting position, pulling his new hostage with him. He wrapped his arm around his neck, tightening his hold. The man struggled, but Lewis was too strong, and a moment later the man went limp.

Lewis needed a plan. He needed one *now*. They would be storming into the bedroom any second. The only advantage he had was the lack of lighting, but of course, that meant he couldn't see shit, either. He didn't have any weapons. All he really had at his disposal was this new hostage. Maybe he could threaten to snap his neck or something if they didn't back off.

Then what? Maybe he'd demand his gun be returned, and his car keys. Get in his car, get as far away from these freaks as possible. Surf the ocean with his beloved heads. Get out of this country once and for all. This had just been a speed bump, nothing more. Soon, he'd be back on the road, heading toward the border.

He heard screaming from the other side of the cabin. People shouting. They were confused, scared. Afraid of the big bad killer on the loose. Lewis smiled. Good, they should be afraid.

Someone, he wasn't sure who, shouted, "Police!" and Lewis's smile faded. Had they really called the cops? That wasn't good. He could outsmart a bunch of dumb writers. But the police were another story. Not that the police were any smarter—they just had more firepower.

Now what was he supposed to do?

"Uh, please don't kill me," a voice said in the darkness.

Lewis jumped. "Who said that?"

"Me," said the voice. He wasn't that far from Lewis's spot on the floor. He sounded close enough to touch.

"Who are you?"

"I'm Jared. I'm an award-winning editor."

"How long have you been in this room?"

"I have no idea where I am. But my head sure does hurt. But listen, if you have any need to hire an editor, maybe we could work something out. I edit for you and you spare my life. What do you think? Any projects opening up?"

"I'm . . . I'm not a writer."

"That doesn't matter."

"Are you with the publishing company, or are you one of those they've abducted?"

"I'm . . . I'm Jared. I just told you that. Blood stings when it gets in your eyes."

"That's true."

"Are you going to kill Nick?"

"Who's Nick?"

"Nick is an asshole."

Lewis thought about it. "I probably will, yeah."

"Can I help?"

42.
Officer Doughnut to the Rescue

"**UN-FUCKING-TIE ME, GODDAMMIT,**" Harlan said. "I'm not going to run away. I just want to defend myself once that psychopath kills the rest of you."

Eliza cut the duct tape from his wrists with the knife she'd snagged from the kitchen.

"That fucker's in there, doing God knows what to him," Louise said. "We gotta go in."

"He might cut your heads off," Harlan said, stretching his newly freed hands.

"With what?" she asked. "Dude doesn't have shit."

"Then how did he free himself?"

"Maybe he's a magician, who knows." Louise stared at the door, quiet for a moment, then she threw her hands up like she was ready to brawl. "Fuck this, let's just charge him."

"Well, Billy has a gun," Eliza said. "Maybe we should—"

The front door burst open. A tall man stormed inside, waving a pistol at them. "Police! Everybody get on the ground!"

They all stood, staring at the man with the gun, confused. Harlan felt a huge weight relieve itself in his stomach, and for a moment he was convinced the weight was a massive turd slipping from his asshole. But alas, it was just stress.

"Finally," Harlan said, smiling.

"Shut up!" the cop said. "Get on the ground!"

They did as they were told.

The cop stared at Louise. "Aren't you the woman who assaulted a child with a muffin today at a Pic-n-Pac?"

"No, that doesn't sound like me."

"Damn, you look familiar."

"Uh, dude?" Louise said. "Just, uh, so you know, there's this serial killer in the other room, and he has my boyfriend hostage. Who knows what he's doing to him."

The cop paused, taking his time to process his words. "Lewis Hill."

"You already know about him?"

The cop—if he even was a cop—seemed to tighten. "He's wanted for the murder of his wife."

"Shit, man, he's killed a lot more than his wife."

Eliza nodded. "There's a whole bunch of severed heads with his name on them. Plus, the bastard murdered our friend."

The cop hesitated before answering, swallowing loudly. "Sergio Placid."

The room was quiet. Then Eliza said, in a whimper, "Oh, Serg."

"We fucked up," Louise said. "We really fucked up."

"And now you're going to prison," Harlan said, almost laughing. "You stupid assholes deserve everything you get."

"Oh fuck you," Louise said.

"Shut up!" the cop shouted, waving his gun. "Stop talking." He nodded at the bedroom. "Is he armed?"

He waited, but nobody responded.

"Goddammit, is Lewis Hill armed? You said he had a hostage?"

Again, the room was quiet.

"What the fuck is wrong with you people?"

"Dude," Louise said. "You told us to stop talking."

"She does have a point," Harlan said.

The cop grunted and kicked Harlan in the side of the head. "You fucking people. This should be a sacred place."

"Who *are* you?" Eliza said.

Harlan tried to sit up, but his head was pounding and the cabin was spinning before his eyes. "Whoever you are, I'm reporting you," he said, and the cop kicked him again. This time he stayed on the floor. There was no reason to sit back up if he was going to get kicked again.

"Is he *armed?*" the cop asked.

"We don't know," Eliza said. "But he's crazy. I saw him kill Sergio. He . . . he was like an animal."

The cop nodded and took off toward the bedroom. He reached out for the door, but it swung open just as he was about to grab the knob. The wooden frame bashed into his face, sending him flying backward into a stack of paperbacks piled on the ground. A candle that'd been resting on top of a stack of books soared across the cabin and landed on another tipped-over pile of books, only it landed upside down, the wax spilling over a sea of scattered pages.

Still on the ground, the cop turned around, raised his pistol, and fired blindly into the dark room. Someone inside screamed.

Everybody held their breath, waiting. Around them, the paperbacks lining the cabin ignited. But nobody seemed to notice but Harlan.

The homeless editor stumbled out of the bedroom, groaning and holding his bloody stomach. "I should have moved to Portland," he said, and collapsed.

"Was that him?" the cop asked, climbing to his feet. "Did I get the sick bastard?"

"Nah, man," Louise said. "That was just Jared."

43.
Politically Correct Decapitations

L EWIS HADN'T NOTICED the window in the bedroom before due to the blinds behind pulled down, but on account of an incredible streak of luck, he accidentally bumped into it. He pulled the blinds up and opened the window. He couldn't believe they'd shot that other guy. The bullet was meant for Lewis, of course. Next time, he wouldn't be so lucky.

His hostage, the one named Stephen, was starting to become more aware of the situation, so he bashed his head into the wall a couple times before pushing him outside. His body made a soft thud as it landed in the dirt. Lewis climbed through and followed him out. The hostage started getting to his feet, but Lewis was on him before he could gain any real distance.

"Not so fast," Lewis whispered, grabbing him by the collar of his shirt and leading him around the cabin. His entire day had been wasted. He was not leaving without at least some kind of reward. This guy had a decent-sized head. Sure, in the past he had only targeted women, but times were different. He needed to not be so sexist. The world was no longer so politically incorrect. His collection could use a little variation. Hell, why limit himself to humans? He could add dogs, cats, fuckin' goats—the sky was the limit.

He would be the king of heads.

He remembered the first time he'd killed somebody. It'd been a complete accident. It was bowling night, so he'd gone out with the boys, drinking and temporarily abandoning responsibility. Afterward, he'd stumbled through the parking lot, drunk and pissed off about his poor bowling skills. A girl was walking around in the dark by herself. She seemed lost, like she needed help, so he offered her a ride. She gladly accepted. Half a mile down the road, she casually mentioned she'd blow him for twenty dollars. He was just drunk enough not to give a shit about consequences, and pulled his truck off on the side of the road. This was back when he still had his truck, before he traded it in, at Helga's request, for something shitty and fuel friendly. He leaned back in the driver's seat and unzipped his jeans. Five minutes later, just as he was on the verge of completion, the girl jammed a gun under his jaw and told him to hand over his wallet. After she stored his wallet in her purse, she ordered him to get out of the truck and begin walking the opposite direction. She said the truck now belonged to her, along with the rest of his bullshit pride. Then a car passed them, and he took the opportunity to knock the gun out of her hand. She freaked out and fled down the road. Lewis chased after her, from behind the wheel. He didn't realize he was going to run her over until her body became a sudden speed bump. Then her corpse was behind him, in the middle of the road, torn to shreds. Fortunately, he kept gardening tools in the back of his truck, including a shovel. As he buried the dead girl in the woods close to where he'd run her over, all he could think about was how his life was ruined, how his reality was shattered. But those feelings had been false. They were just fears planted by the media. Thoughts he was told he was supposed to think. In truth, he kind of felt good. Hell, he felt great. And when he dumped her body in the shallow hole and stabbed the shovel into her throat, he felt goddamn amazing.

Lewis would not allow some imbecile writers to stop him from continuing his destiny. He would kill until God himself descended from the heavens and put him down like a rabid dog.

He continued around the cabin, hungry to retrieve his collection. Up ahead, the man named Nick stood in front of the building. For a moment, Lewis thought he didn't see him, that he was shielded by darkness, his one true ally. But that fantasy was destroyed when Nick raised Lewis's own gun and shot him.

44.
Authors, Reviewers & Serial Killers

NICK HAD SHOT the serial killer but the serial killer didn't seem fazed. They just stood there, glaring at each other. Stephen stood to the side of Lewis, exhausted and defeated. Lewis held him by his shirt collar. Yet he wasn't shot. Or at least, he didn't look like he was shot.

Then Nick realized he'd missed.

"Shit," he said, and fired the gun again.

Stephen screamed and fell to the ground, clutching his knee.

"Fuck," Nick said, and tried again.

Not even close.

Lewis tackled him before he could get off another shot. The gun flew from his hand. Nick hit the ground hard. The world vibrated and he forgot how to breathe for a moment. Lewis sat on his stomach and pounding into his face.

Was Lewis growling?

Shit, he was a dead man. Nick couldn't fight. He couldn't even move. He should have ran when he still had the chance.

Somewhere, miles away, Stephen was crying about his knee.

Nick smelled smoke. He wondered if he was smelling death. His own death. He turned his head to the side, saw the cabin. It was on fire. It was beautiful. Lewis punched him again. Everything was spinning. He missed Sergio. He missed his parents. He wanted to go home. He wondered if that publishing company had read *The Owls in the City* yet. They probably hated it.

Someone shouted, then Lewis fell off Nick's stomach. Nick focused his eyes, saw Harlan standing above him. He was holding a severed head, gripping it by the long, black hair connected to the scalp.

Nick meant to say "Harlan", but it came out as "Jesus?"

"Shut up," Harlan said. He stepped over Nick and moved to Lewis. He raised the severed head and swung it at him, then swung it again, bashing it into his face.

"That's for grabbing my dick!" Harlan shouted, and hit him once more. Lewis lay on the ground, motionless. "And for letting me get kidnapped! And for not telling me I spent half the goddamn day next to a bag of heads! And this is for all the shitty literature in the world! You fuck! You mother*fuck*!"

Harlan didn't stop swinging the head until Nick pulled him away.

Nick felt weak, his face bloody and aching. He looked at Harlan, watched him panting, trying to catch his breath. He was still holding the head.

"You saved me," Nick said. "Thank you."

"Oh, fuck you and your press," Harlan said, and bashed the deformed head into Nick's face.

He didn't exactly pass out, but he certainly didn't get back up once he fell down. He simply did not possess enough energy to move.

He heard Harlan open a car door, then close it. The engine was already running. The guy who'd showed up to the cabin with a gun, he'd left his car running like a dumbass.

HOW TO SUCCESSFULLY KIDNAP STRANGERS

Harlan drove away, leaving Nick down for the count and the cabin in flames.

Nick's pocket vibrated.

He pulled out his cellphone, opened his email. He had one new message in his inbox:

Dear Nick,

Thank you for submitting *The Owls in the City* . . .

45.
Fahrenheit 451

HEY WERE SURROUNDED by hundreds of
Sergio's books, all of them burning. Sergio always
told Eliza one day his books would be burned,
although in his head he had pictured a bunch of whacko
Christians being the pyros. This worked, too, though.

Eliza stood up, coughing, the smoke strangling her
lungs. Inside the bedroom, the cop was saying there was
nobody else here. Eliza and Louise walked in, now able to
see thanks to the flames preparing to swallow them
whole.

"Where the fuck did they go?" Louise said, then spotted
the open window. She pointed, excited. "Shit, they
escaped!" She ran for the window and climbed out.

The cop pointed his gun and told her to stop, she was
still under arrest.

Louise laughed. "Fuck you, copper. I have to save my
boyfriend."

She leapt outside and took off into the forest, shouting
Stephen's name.

Eliza and the cop stood in the burning cabin for a
moment, shrugging.

"Well," he said, "I suppose we ought to get out of here
before we burn to death."

Eliza nodded. "Good plan."

HOW TO SUCCESSFULLY KIDNAP STRANGERS

Outside, Nick sat in the dirt, his face illuminated by the glow of his cell phone. He was laughing like a crazy person.

The cop glanced around, confused. "Where the fuck is my car?"

Eliza kicked her editor-in-chief. "Calm down, man. You're losing it."

Nick shook his head, still laughing. Laughing so hard he was crying. He held up his cell phone, showing her the screen. She read it, then started laughing too.

"Congratulations," she said, and their laughter spiraled further out of control. "You're gonna have to write the sequel on toilet paper rolls."

Nick abruptly stopped laughing and looked at her, serious. "I have to write a sequel?"

46.

How to Successfully Kidnap Kidnappers

HARLAN HAD DRIVEN ten minutes before he realized Billy was sitting in the backseat.

"So, where are we going?" the tweaker asked.

Harlan screamed, slammed on the brakes. Billy bashed his face against the driver's seat.

"Shit, man, I didn't have my seatbelt on."

Harlan sat behind the wheel for a moment, breathing heavily, trying to avoid a heart attack. Then he got out, opened the back door, and pulled Billy from the passenger seat, dragging him out in the road.

"Hey, man, what the fuck are you doing?"

Harlan didn't respond, just kept dragging him around the car. He popped open the trunk.

Billy laughed nervously. "You can't be serious."

Harlan pushed him inside and closed the trunk, then got back behind the wheel and started driving again. He no longer felt pain. His body had numbed, blissful and content. Harlan drove into the night, aching to get back home and write a new blog post.

This was going to be his best one yet.

ABOUT THE AUTHOR

Max Booth III is a novelist, screenwriter, editor, podcaster, and publisher. He is the author of *Abnormal Statistics, Maggots Screaming!, Touch the Night*, and many other titles too spooky to name here. His film, *We Need to Do Something*, was released by IFC Midnight in 2021. With his wife, Lori, he co-runs Ghoulish Books, a small press and indie bookstore based in San Antonio, Texas. Learn more about him at TalesFromTheBooth.com.

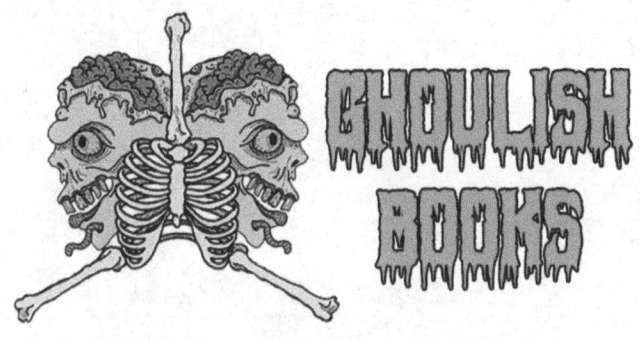

Patreon:
www.patreon.com/ghoulishbooks

Website:
www.Ghoulish.rip

Facebook:
www.facebook.com/GhoulishBooks

Twitter:
@GhoulishBooks

Instagram:
@GhoulishBookstore

Linktree:
linktr.ee/ghoulishbooks